Rotten Row

Rotten Row

Chaz Brenchley

2011

Rotten Row

Copyright © Chaz Brenchley 2011

Cover

Copyright © Christopher Walker 2011

First Edition

ISBN
978-1-848632-11-0
978-1-848632-12-7 (Signed Edition)

Design and Layout by Aaron Leis.
Printed and bound in England by the MPG Books Group.
Set in Centaur

PS Publishing Ltd.
Grosvenor House
1 New Road
Hornsea, HU18 1PG
England

editor@pspublishing.co.uk
www.pspublishing.co.uk

Rotten Row

This is for Liz Williams.
I went looking for her, and found this instead.
It's a gift.

Heading outward is heading onward; your journey never needs to end. Every step falls just one short of another, and why wouldn't you want to take it? As it's there?

We call them terminals, but that's only legacy, it's a label. Nothing terminates. A 'chute supplies another node; it's a link in the network, not a destination. It can always fling you further, somewhere else. That's the law, or else it's the guiding principle. You never need to go back.

And then there's Rotten Row.

They call it that, those who live there, those who choose. Us, the rest of us, the Upshot and the downsiders, for once united: those who know enough to be afraid? We call it the Terminus.

Rotten Row is a loop, a lap, a circuit in itself. It's also a dead end, the defiance of all law and custom. It's not connected; there's nowhere else to go. You go out, you come back.

While you're there, while you're looping, you can defy all the other laws of the Upshot. Why not? Whatever you do there, stays there. You can't bring it back into the network.

Think of a wheel that spins around a notional axis on an absent hub. It doesn't need a centre; it doesn't actually need spokes, though it has them. Two of them, pointing not quite directly at each other.

One of those, of course, is the Upchute: universal friend to the home-free, the body-free, the wilful wanderer. Friend to all of us who want to come and stay a while and then move on. Try something new, be someone different, shift and shift again. Jump from one discard to the next, travel the network, see more of human space, never be quite the same person twice.

The other? That's heresy, corruption, breach. They call it the Downchute. Not quite so long, not quite so straight, not standard: it's the inescapable symbol of how wrong they are, wrong-headed and wrong-bodied on the Row.

They can leave, of course, at any time. They can come back to the community, to a proper discard and the rule of law. They're there by choice, though, and they tend to stay. That's the offence, the sin, the unforgivable. Choosing neither the downside nor the Upshot but this offshoot, alien to both; stepping aside from humanity, breaking what was promised and going nowhere, turning and turning, turning on themselves . . .

I came to Rotten Row from NeoPenthe, necessarily. That's inherent. There is no other way to come. They still have manual checking at departure, for reasons that became obvious as soon as I gave my destination. The clerk looked at me askance—if a bitter contempt can be contained in such a euphemistic word—and asked me why.

"Do I need to tell you?"

"That's for you to say. You don't *have* to tell me; I'll send you anyway. Whether you *need* to spill it, for your own comfort or whatever reason else, that's your choice. I'm just sitting here doing my job, and a sister who seems otherwise healthy and intelligent is asking me to send her to the worst place we've made, the worst place we ever will make, and I do feel the need to ask."

"Don't worry," I said, "I'll be back." Trying a smile and seeing it lost entirely in that little space between my goodwill and her repugnance. "I just need to go there, I need to *see* . . ."

"There are broadcasts," she said, curling her lip. "Constantly. You can sit in your room and *see*."

Oh, I could. Her voice suggested that she had. I was sure of it. Being so topologically close, NeoPenthe the only transit-point to Rotten Row, no doubt everyone on the station had *seen* in that official authorised Awful Warning way, that tone of voice the whole station had adopted. No doubt there were indoctrination sessions for their children; no doubt their adolescents hacked into uncensored channels for thrillfests in the dark. None of that was any use to me.

"I'm an artist," I said. "Full-immersion protocols." Chances were, that would mean nothing to her. As a form it was local, born downside on my own system, and it hadn't spread. No surprise. When your whole culture is paranoid about identity, anything that seeks or serves to place you within someone else's experience is suspect by definition. The Upshot as a class would not touch immer, and the Upshot were the only means by which art or information could leapfrog from one system to another. That I had needed to take the 'chute myself in pursuit of my own practice, that I needed to chase that practice further and further across human space, that was nothing but irony. I still had to go home or homeabouts to work, and to exhibit.

Still, I said it anyway, I announced myself; and then I cursed myself silently for sounding so much like a sophisticate on tour to the hicks. In response to her blankness, though, I had nothing to do but carry on. "I want to make a work about Rotten Row, about endings, dead ends, evolutionary killing-zones. I can't do it, unless I've been there. Actually been, in the body. Virtual experience is no use to me. Nor is viral, someone else's tales, broadcast or whispered one-to-one . . ."

She shrugged. "That's what they all say, more or less. They need to feel it, taste it, smell it for themselves. Being an artist, that's new, but you're all tourists to me," and her face said quite clearly how she felt about that, about us, all of us who went to Rotten Row.

No blame to her; she's right, more or less. Pretty much everyone who goes there is a tourist first, avid for experience, for that hint of decadence in their life-story: "Oh yes, I've been to the Terminus. To Rotten Row. Fascinating. So rich, so wrong—but my dear, so rich . . ."

Not me, but I couldn't explain, I could never persuade her. She had her position: pure orthodoxy, except that she'd think herself and all the community well shot of me and all my kind, if I and we would only choose to stay on Rotten Row.

Some did, of course. That would be, surely must be an aspect of any piece I made. It was what I couldn't understand, what I needed to discover: why anyone would choose a closed system, a deliberate decay, no future.

Fever or passion or terror, whatever it was that gripped them, I didn't expect to catch it. I couldn't imagine that it was infectious; also, I was very sure it wouldn't travel. No one need fear evangelists coming back to preach temptation. If you'd found what you wanted somewhere in the ferment, in the crucible of the Terminus, your first step back would be the uttermost loss.

Besides, if anyone tried to speak for Rotten Row, if proselytising carried any weight at all, the Upshot would never allow them out.

Sometimes, it's hard to remember that to downsiders we're the pirates, the wild ones, the anarchs. In practice, Upshot law is absolute among us, and the constant remedy is death.

Or flight, I suppose, if you could manage it, if you were quick; and the Terminus would be the swiftest place to fly to, one location where Upshot writ won't run. One thing for sure, if you could only get there, no one would ever try to follow you in.

Sometimes you wait a long time, at a 'chute. The network's busy all over: at any node people are always arriving, leaving, passing through. And whatever the pressure, they can still only process one discard at a time, coming or going. You get delays. Everywhere, you get delays.

walk; and you can't rely on the body to find its own way to balance because it's new, it's fresh, unworn, it's never done this yet. But there are people on hand to steer you to a sideroom, to mirrors and manuals—orientation materials, local laws and tendencies if you choose to go downside—and clothes that fit perfectly because of course they knew all the dimensions of this neutral-smelling discard just decanted from the growing vats. Dressing is difficult, with fingers and fashions both unfamiliar, but willing hands will help; and there's a mall nearby where you can shop at will for clothes that suit you better, suit your sense of self if not your sudden colouring. There's a gym where you can exercise this body and get it used to moving, get it used to you. There's a universal chapel, should you need to pray or bless yourself or dedicate this body to whatever faith you've brought with you. As a community, the Upshot don't tend towards the religious—it's reckoned hard to believe in a creator-god when your every body is created for you and worn like clothes and discarded like clothes when you're done with it, left behind for filing—but we are by definition a community of exceptions, the ones who walked away. Those who do cling to faith reckon that what we do is almost prayerful in itself, that flinging our selves from one body to the next is absolute proof that the human soul exists in separation from any corporeal function.

Praying or shopping or working out, all the time you're meeting other people, locals and incomers like yourself. Little is automated and nothing is private; you pick up customs, styles, news, that general sense of being somewhere else yet still entirely among your own kind. However alien the world beyond the terminal—if there is one, if this isn't an orbital station—and however far you've come, the Upshot are as determinedly uniform as the 'chutes themselves. You left a world of human-normal, and you come into just such another. Every discard is generated from unmodified human code, random but utterly reliable, no sports or freaks or alterations.

And then there's Rotten Row.

Out of the pod. That inescapable blink upward, up and up, the slow curve of the 'chute's rise and the haze that hides whatever lies above, that field or force that can punch information through some mysterious otherspace, give it distance and direction, let it find another 'chute for download, not instantaneous but close enough for maths; and then—dizzy from that brutal scaling, or from the fling, or from whatever malfunction might have delayed it—the stagger towards the door as it slides open.

And already, by the stretch and weight of that stagger, I know that there's been no malfunction. This is not the body I had before. So I'm looking down and finding myself male, not hirsute but dark-haired, lightly framed but still taller, heavier, longer-legged than the female I'd so briefly been on NeoPenthe. Perhaps I'm lightly, pointlessly cursing the paranoia that drives us into randomised bodies, to relearn our own selves at every fling. There is no evading this: Downsiders insist on it, and the whole structure of Upshot society is built around it. When a body can be grown to exact specifications and a mind—or soul, or personality, whatever it is that we Upshot are—can be passed from one to another, identity becomes a dangerously fluid concept. A man walks into the 'chute, and takes the fling. We can grow him a new body in his absence, from his own DNA; what we can't do, we cannot guarantee that the person flung back into it is the same person that left before. In the absence of science, then, we have paranoia. We have to divorce identity from recognition. If you can't trust a familiar face, a voice, the touch of known hands returning, better then to outlaw them. It is forbidden to grow any body to order, to a known pattern. Those of us who take the fling go blindly from one discard, one random body to another. Behind us is a data-trail, everything known and recorded, our scattered chain of bodies crushed and kept as evidence, little cakes of carbon; ahead is nothing but uncertainty, mutability, the luck of the draw. We prove ourselves in countless ways to be ourselves, but those are never physical.

Which is why we must blunder about in unfamiliar skins every time we take the fling, suddenly the wrong height and weight, often the wrong gender; and why I'm not at all paying attention to my surroundings at the Terminus until my eye snags on a scratch in the plass flooring and my ear's caught by a voice close beside.

You can't scratch plass. That's an absolute. It's one of those certainties we build our lives upon. Like the law that says no Upshot may ever have a choice, which body they're flung into: that it shall be a body grown from pure human DNA with random markers, one use only, recorded and discarded.

And then there's Rotten Row.

Where plass is casually scratchable, apparently, and where a voice may say something entirely normal—"Easy, now; how are you feeling, can I help?"—but the tone of it is so strange, like a harsh chime of bells, it can take a moment even to understand that as a sentence, let alone to pick out the sense of it.

I did do that, but a beat behind my eyes. I heard him before I saw him, and I saw him before I understood him.

He was tall in a way that I was not, that no true-human legal Upshot discard ever could be: half a metre taller than me, even before I figured in his crest.

That was feathers, or feathery tissue of some kind, erupting from the hairless, scaly skin of his scalp. It had colours—green and blue and silver, largely—that would have looked bright anywhere, were positively gaudy against the neutral tones of plass; and it added another half-metre to his apparent height, before it fell away down his back.

He dressed to match his colours, a silver jumpsuit piped with seams of jade. His hands were apparently human-normal, except for a snaky scaliness that gave them too a shimmer of greenish colour; his feet belonged on a bird, I thought, heavily scaled with three great splayed toes on each. I looked at the black steel claws that tipped them and imagined what those might do to plass if he really tried to dig them in, wondered whatever could have happened here to make him do that thing.

I looked at clothes, hands, feet, because shocking as they were, all of them together were still easier than looking at his face.

Perhaps we don't realise just how indoctrinated we are. Among the Upshot there's a variety—not infinite but absolute, the entire range—of human types, more so than any downside race can manage; there is not, ever, any modification beyond the human. I had learned from the earliest, as we all do, that this was abomination. I had been reminded explicitly whenever I'd studied the subject of Rotten Row, every time I'd raised it. And now here it was in all its flaunted hybrid flesh, and it was very hard to look upon.

Flesh and feathers, flesh and skin and—

Well, beak. Something beak-like, at least, that deformed the lower half of his face and thrust at me, making those sounds that I was only now interpreting as words, a stare and a gasp too late.

His eyes were big and round and bird-bright, ringed with colour: fur or tiny feathers, hard to say. It was still the beak that snared me. It lacked the full yellow clacking maw of a bird, and yet it had left a human face and jawline far behind. There were open nostrils and then a hooking curve, scales blending into something bonebare, a sheen more like oyster than mother-of-pearl. When it opened to let him speak again in that chiming grate he had, I saw teeth that were more or less human, a tongue that was emphatically not.

"Easy, I said! You can't be that shaken, I know they warned you before you came up the line. Here, let me . . ."

There was strength in those hands of his; he must have at least human-normal muscles under the jumpsuit. That at least. He had sensitivity too, though, in his head if not in his fingers. He let me shrug him off easily enough.

Even shrugging felt strange, in these new shoulders. Still, "I can manage," I mumbled, trying out the new voice to go with the old manners, graceless as ever.

"Not sure you can. But you are allowed to try. This way, then," and he strutted towards a side-wall, long stiff legs that I couldn't hope to keep up with.

This was what I'd come for, or the first dry taste of it, a hint on the breeze, a promise. That he left me awkward in his wake, struggling to follow, staring as he went: that, too, was what I had come for. I'd said *to see*, but *to watch* would have been more truthful. Active observation, reaching to absorb. That was the ideal. In practice, unsurprisingly, struggling to follow.

He strutted, I shambled, we came through a door to a dressing-room. A high broad door, fit to accommodate his height and the crest of him above that, fit to accommodate five of him side by side, or one five times as wide: another measure of how different this place was, constructed with inhuman bodies in mind. The clothes he'd laid out for me were neutral cut and neutral colours, shrieking *tourist*, *voyeur* against the blaze of him. No doubt my entire body would shriek the same message, however I dressed it. Perhaps there were people here who lived muted lives, unmodified—but what would be the point of that, where was the attraction? You came to see, or else to be; there was no visible purpose in the journey, else.

If anyone was actually born here, if there were genuine native children—but I didn't want to think about that. I didn't need to. I decided not to ask.

"You want the mirror yet?"

I was getting used to his voice, or at least learning to pick the words out of it. "Please, yes."

No shimmer of a reflective field here, responding to a finger's pressure on a stud. He opened a closet door, and there was a physical looking-glass. Full-length, fit to show the whole of me with plenty of room all around.

Tawny-brown skin, but I knew that already. A strong determined face, I liked that, beneath black hair unusually close-cropped. Most terminals would leave it long, just as it came from the tank, for us to cut and style as we chose. Sometimes a planetary station would conform to downside custom for the sake of local peace, but that was rare.

He had to help me, with buttons and ties. I didn't have fine control of my fingers yet. After the last delicate pair of hands, I wasn't sure I would ever achieve much that was fine with these broad paddles; but that was a familiar loss of perspective, that always needed a day or two to recover. Going the other way, male to female, I could feel almost too fragile to move. Besides the adjustment to a different engineering, and the shifts of different hormones in my blood. Watching your own personality change between one terminal and the next, it's a constant fascination for the Upshot; understanding how the core, the person beneath the personality never changes at all, that's a cause of theses without number. Downsiders have reasons to call us self-obsessed.

While he buttoned me up, he said, "We like newcomers to be greeted by a morph. Nothing too extreme, but nothing subtle either. Not so that you could ignore it. It's important to make the point: this is what we do, what we're about. Why we're here. And you, if you've come to look at us, you might as well start now. If you're interested in staying, you might as well see straight away what kind of community you'll be joining. Anything else would be deception. Some people find it hard, I know—but they'd find it worse to be greeted by straight human and then blunder straight out into the Row. They come here wanting a gradual introduction, they make a real fuss about it sometimes when they see us—but that's what they're getting, truly. Just enough to make it real. In your case, what you get is me."

He said, "No, honestly. I'm moderate, as morphs go. You call us morphs, or modified, or whatever you like. We call ourselves the Farflung, and I'm not half as far as some. Not yet. I've gone twice now, end to end—that's what we call it; you'll pick up the language soon enough, that's the easy part—and I've another body brewing as we speak. With wings, and a lot more feathers."

He said, "The wings are just vestigial, first time through. You have to develop, oh, mental muscles. The habit of wings. Or six legs, or whatever. You're all right in a straight human body, it only takes a day to adjust; but say you'd come out of the 'chute with an extra pair of arms, how would you use them? The mentation's not there, you've got no access. Minds are conservative, they cling to what they know, what they started with. The same way, if you lose a limb, your mind still thinks it's there? Grow an extra limb, you have no idea what to do with it. You have to learn. So next time I get little stubs, and learn to flap them. Eventually I'll have wings fit to fly—but that could be a long time yet. I'm working with a mentor, she's fabulous, but strict. Won't let me get ahead of myself, says she's seen too many broken birds . . ."

Too many broken dreams would be another way to say it, and I was sure that he was right. She was right. I was glad he had someone to watch over him, stop him over-reaching.

His name was Tethys. He stayed with me, showed me around reception and did his best to see that I understood it. He took me shopping, and to eat; and to an exercise-hall, where he quietly allowed me to ogle him and others quite unlike him, all of them stripped and variously gorgeous and very far from naked in their furs or fancy skins or plumage.

It's exhausting enough, simply to learn the limits of a body that's newly out of the tank. Add in the wonder and the weirdness of these—can I call them people?—who made bodies for themselves, out here in the Terminus, and I was in some place beyond exhaustion, beyond exertion, almost beyond any ability to come back.

When I asked him which way to a pharmacy, when I said I needed drugs, he almost rebelled.

"What for? If you're not adjusting I can fetch you a medic, but you seem good to me. If it's just recreational, you really don't need that. It's sleep you need, not stimulation."

Ordinarily, he'd be right. But, "I told you I'm an artist," I said. "I need the drugs for my work, and I need to start them now, before I go out on the Row."

Even here, I was safe to find everything I wanted. Sometimes a fling goes wrong, that obscure marriage between data-stream and discard just won't take, and there's no alternative to intervention. The drugs they use are crucial to my work; it's my good fortune that they are accessible to me in my life. At least, without them my work, my life would have developed another way. It's art that we're born to, not form.

Those of us who live the way we do, the Upshot community, we who fling ourselves from body to body in pursuit of new stars and new opportunities: for survival's sake, for coherence, to hold our selves together we build a mental shell around our character. It takes a while and we make mistakes, but after the first dozen flings, we tend to have a very coherent sense of self that nothing, almost nothing can batter at.

I have to break that down, if I'm to work. I have to find an empathic path to others' experience, a way to meld their feelings with my vision, a way to breach the wall. They have to infect me, against all the protections that I've grown or set in place.

I use drugs to make this happen. Those drugs that will save a desperate mind from rejecting its host body, from turning inward into psychosis and withdrawal, will allow me deliberately to break down my own security: to make myself vulnerable to influence, to find truth in the beauty of an alien perspective.

It's a hard thing to do to oneself. Sometimes I wonder if it's a harder thing to watch. It troubles people always, all the Upshot, who understand something of what I'm doing. They anticipate the dangers, and none of the rewards; they've never seen my work, never will see it and would never understand it if they did.

To see me do it fresh from the 'chute, when I'm unbalanced anyway, already half adrift, that must be harder yet. To feel the urge to stop me, and to have no right.

I do know what I do to other people. That's my work. Part of my work. You can never take the artist from the art.

Tethys took me where I asked, and stayed with me; watched me take the drugs, asked the usual questions. Was baffled and disturbed in the usual way, never mind how much his own choices baffled and disturbed me. I wanted to offer him comfort, something more than words, but we were misreading each other already; the drugs couldn't salvage that, and none of my instincts was reliable. Swapping discards, especially when you swap genders, you get confused between memory and desire. He was male, inhumanly beautiful, rampantly sexual—like a bird, indeed, which would have pleased him mightily, I thought, which might have provided a basis for mutual pleasure—and besides, I was deeply curious about those feathers. I wanted the touch of them, the taste of them, textures on my tongue. More. But not these first hours outflung, so far from any safe ground.

Even so, I couldn't stay in reception. The drugs wouldn't be biting yet, but everything else was: the vulnerability of a new body, the transgressive nature of this society, the urgency of arrival. I needed contact and exposure; I needed to touch bottom, to test the limits of what I was embracing here. To test my own prejudice, perhaps, while I could still claim it mine.

Tethys tried to persuade me to stay longer, to go slower, even to sleep awhile. If I could manage it without more drugs. When he couldn't shift me, when he saw that I was determined, he brought me to a standard human stairway, winding down.

"That's the shortest way down onto the Row," he said. "I'd help with your bags, but, well . . ."

His broad clawed feet, his gesture said, they were the problem: not shaped for stairs this narrow or this steep. I smiled, thanked him, swore that I could manage. Hefted my new bags with my new clothes in, everything else I needed—you learn to travel light, when you start with nothing and leave with nothing and start again, again—and set off down.

All to the good, perhaps, to be doing this alone. As I went, my feelings seemed to cycle backwards, out of the daze of wonder. Beak, claws—what had I been thinking? There was a shudder in me now, just at the notion. That was good, though, I could use it. Indeed, that was the limit of usefulness, absolutely what I'd come for: to find that balance-point between attraction and its opposite, to step up close but draw back. Art stops short of entanglement, necessarily. The other thing's pornography.

That was how I felt, on the stairs there: touched by porn, eroticised at random. Except that 'random' was the wrong word here. Discards are assigned at random, that's the law, that's how it works—and then there's Rotten Row. Here they choose their bodies, they *design* them. Plot them out and nurture them, watch them grow, forced in the tanks. Decants they call them, not discards; the wealthy have them lined up, fine bodies waiting, hurry hurry.

The poor save or work, borrow or beg, indenture themselves in pursuit of funds for their next. It's aspirational.

Rotten Row is a wheel, a lap. By definition it ought to go nowhere. How it works, though, they have two 'chutes. They can toss themselves from one to the other, from one designer body to the next, as often as they choose. And still go nowhere, but who cares? Why would they ever want to leave?

It's insular, inverted, masturbatory. They know that. That's what I wanted to watch here, what I'd come in search of: the self-knowledge, the addiction, the sour point below the shriek.

Tourists never see it. Nor do the commentators, the legislators, the moral philosophers, the appalled. What every visitor sees, what gets recorded and transmitted home for Awful Warnings and tourist-bait and, yes, pornography—that's the lap itself, the parade, the Row in all its plumage.

You make your way through reception and there are morphs, Farflung, the body-modified everywhere you look: some subtly altered from a human norm, some less subtly so, some not subtle at all. In your face, in your eye, in your head. At first it's hard to look; then it's hard not to stare; then you give up and just stare anyway. That's what they want, anyway. Why do this to themselves, if not to be stared at?

And you know, because they tell you, that these are still the moderates among the remade. You could call them Mods—for moderate, for modified, for both—if they didn't so determinedly call themselves by other names. Out there, they say, on the Row: that's where the action is, that's where the real people are. We're picked for this, they say, for reception-duty, because we make it easy on you.

As they flash their crests and fluff their fur, blink their one eye or their third eye, reach to scratch with that so-useful extra hand.

And it's true, you know that; it is true. You've seen the broadcasts. You know what's waiting for you out there, beyond that quiet unheraldic exit door at the foot of all those stairs.

You think you know. You may have spent an hour on the open balcony above, pointing, questioning, staring down. Cushioned by distance, yes, but still. You think you know.

And then you take the stairs, come to the door, step through. All of that, and then there's Rotten Row.

You're on the Row, and this is what you came for, and it's . . . immense. Immersive. Terrifying, in the way that only one thing, your first tentative step into the Upshot community has been before. You left your birth-body behind, that thing that had so defined you up till now; you thought that was the biggest step you'd ever make or need to make, in your head or otherwise.

And then you came to Rotten Row.

Aliens you're used to, surely, if you've come this far. Terminals and 'chutes are human-specific, human only, but there are other species all around us. You can't get here without passing though other people's yards; you can't pass through without pausing, looking, lingering. It's the alien-in-human that jars: hybridity, perversion, the sudden apprehension in the flesh.

You thought you were ready, before you came. Then you met reception.

You survived reception, and adjusted. Again you thought you were ready, and you clattered down every single one of those stairs—on foot, of course, and alone unless you came with a party, unless you waited for them—and finally you stepped through the door.

Did you vomit, did you run back up? Did you fugue? People do. Shame is your own concern; no one here will care. They're used to it, and utterly uninterested in tourists except as a source of income. Which makes them highly interested, I suppose, but still brutally unconcerned. It may be that's a part of the show, to be as proud and scornful as they are beautiful, as they are deformed, as they are deranged.

Rotten Row is a wheel that rolls and rolls, a spinning hoop in orbit around a dead planet, a cinder that offers nothing but its gravity. The Row has no use, no function, no gaze beyond itself. There are no windows looking outward.

The inside rim of the wheel makes a road, broad and unbroken, one long lap twice straddled by the separate 'chutes. That road of course is the Row proper, unless the Row is the parade. Or the people who parade it.

Say it's the road, let's keep this simple.

Reception is an arch above the road—there are windows looking down, there is that deceptive balcony, but it's too high up to show you much beyond the dark attractive ribbon and the glitter of its setting, the movement of little creatures far below. The view is a lure, no more: *come on down.* The 'chute of course is invisible above that, thrusting up and out, almost breaching the seal of this atmospheric world.

Out of the door, aching after so many stairs; out of the door and straight onto the Row. No wonder people fugue.

Actually, to be fair, there is a sidewalk and a rail to keep you from stepping straight into the parade. Just, the sidewalk is narrow and the rail is slender, and neither one is anything like enough.

The parade isn't a scheduled event; it's a constant, an actuality. Where they walk, the Farflung, they parade. That's what they're here for.

What I was here for, too: that vanity, that self-absorption, the sense that art and awareness are the same. That the one can satisfy the other. I knew I could make something of this.

I stood there and saw creatures come by me, not only that I couldn't name; creatures I couldn't even describe, even to myself as I was watching. It wasn't simply the words I lacked, it was the concepts. They stood before me and I still couldn't imagine such beings, such shapes, such lives. There were portions I could recognise—limbs, skin, features—and proportions too, so that my mind might falter between human and elephantine, human and lupine, human and hart; but too often it broke completely in the disjunct between what was surely human once and what had never been. Again, I had seen these things on screens before I came, but that was nothing. This was too too solid, and impossible to process.

"Hey. Staying?"

Oddly, it was a relief to be spoken to, even from a parade of monsters. Even if the question seemed at once inevitable and impossible. She was in the corner of my eye; I turned sharply and here was another relief, that I had a word I could apply to her. To all of her, from her short-cropped hair to her scrawny hindquarters.

And to the jitney, the two-wheeled cab she was harnessed to. That was a rickshaw, and she was a centaur. No question about it. The full deal: horse's body—or pony's, perhaps, it was too lightly framed and too short in the back to be truly horse—and her own torso rising above, young and fit and female, fine-boned and attractive.

She wore a breastband, for the sake of politeness unless it was convenience, and nothing else except the harness. From the waist on down—down and back—she didn't need to, of course. Her dark coat was the exact same shade as her hair, and gave her a dense animal decency that only made her human part look more naked and exposed.

"Oh—no," I stammered, "no, I'm not staying. Just here to observe . . ."

"No, I mean, where are you staying? Hotel?"

I hadn't thought that far. I was still staring, it was taking all my time.

"Hey. You could stare just as well from my rick."

"I don't know where to—"

"No, but I do. Before you're done staring, you'll be there. Nice room, view of the Row, just what you're looking for."

I'd already found what I was looking for; and, "I don't think I'll ever be done staring."

Here came a—a man, call him a man; he had two penises and he was wearing them right out front, to make sure that everybody knew. Briefly I thought that was short-sighted, because human bodies weren't built to accommodate such generosity; but this was Rotten Row, and bodies could be rebuilt to suit. Likely he'd find someone willing, for money or less fungible assistance, perhaps just for the adventure of it. If not—well, this was Rotten Row. *Look at me!* might be enough for him; perhaps they weren't meant for use. It's all about the parade.

Genitalia were the least of his alterations, in any case. In simple glamour terms, they were. In profligacy. They were flung forward into prominence by the way he stood, the way he moved; that was conditioned by something he'd had done to his pelvis and hips, so that his legs bent backwards. Like a bird's: something my friend Tethys from last night hadn't thought of, or didn't want, or more likely couldn't afford. Wings must come expensive, even if they weren't load-bearing yet. There would be sacrifices, compromises, deals.

This guy wasn't bird-fixated, though. He'd take what offered. No wings for him, no plumage. He had scales, more stegosaur than snake, great clashing plates of armour on his back with a ridge of spines for decorative pleasure. Or for protection. People who would do this to themselves, do it again and again, what might they not do to each other . . . ?

It was the kind of question my drugs were meant to help me with. I could feel them biting like acid at my own protection, breaking it down, leaving me vulnerable and exposed to a dangerous, compulsive understanding.

My centaur-cabby stamped her foot, one of her rear hooves, entirely horse-like. At the same time, entirely human, she said, "You still need somewhere to stay. And you don't want to walk it, fresh from the 'chute, you know you don't; and I can take you somewhere good, better and cheaper than you'd find yourself. And, well, I need the fare."

That at least I could believe. Her morph was looking quite modest, compared to the wild extravagances being paraded behind her; and she was working here rather than parading, finding a way to use what she had. And she was too skinny, both halves of her, she looked wholly hungry . . .

Even so, "Are those the only two choices?" I asked. "Walk, or ride with you?"

"Oh, there are others who'll sell you a ride," she admitted. "You're in the right place for it. Every few minutes, one of us comes by here. You can wait for the next cab that offers; you can wait all day, if you just want to gawp awhile. But they'll keep bothering you, we pitch for fares here. If you want to see the Row undisturbed, you're better in a cab."

"I meant, no mechanical transport? No beltways, no shuttles . . . ?"

"Oh. No, nothing like that. Not much that's mechanised at all, on the Row. We can't afford it."

All their resources went into body modification, she meant, and sustaining a second 'chute. Some of the Row's more extreme inhabitants were wealthy, for meanings of wealth that encompassed whole planetary systems; even so, there must be an economy outside patronage, and that economy must depend on income from elsewhere. Which must meant tourism, largely, though I was sure there were other and darker trades here too.

I thought she was admirable, I thought she was pitiable, hitched to her wagon and towing people about for cash. That no doubt she hoarded against the next due instalment on her next body.

There was no way I could refuse her. By any definition but my own, I was a tourist here, with more money than I needed. The bags I carried were testament to it, all my recent shopping; in truth, my simple presence was testament enough, but the bags were better. Without that conspicuous consumption I might have been the other thing, a supplicant in search of my own first morph.

They use simple plass tokens on Rotten Row, as a medium of exchange. I did the classic tourist thing, holding out a few of them on my palm and asking how many she wanted. She tutted, picked out a small one and told me to put the rest away.

"What's your name?" I asked, climbing into the cab.

She was quite astonishingly flexible, bending to pick up my bags and twisting at the waist to pass them back across her narrow withers.

"Mel's good for me," she said. "Mel-2, technically, but you needn't trouble with that."

"I didn't know they cloned here," I said, startled, meaning *even here* but managing—just—not to say it. Cloning had been proscribed for centuries. I supposed it would lie quite comfortably with what else went on at Rotten Row, but—

"Don't," she said. "Not even here," with a grin over her shoulder that gave weight to every word. "People here want to be unique. Like you. Just, not random, y'know?"

Most clearly, not random. The cab's poles hung from a yoke across her shoulders; she put her hands to them for extra grip, and clicked to herself in some ironic gesture at the long millennia of human interaction with horses.

The wheels had pneumatic tyres; there was barely a sound below the steady clopping of her hooves, as she filtered into the unhurried traffic of the Row. I said, "So what makes you Mel-2, if you're not a clone? Who's Mel-1?"

"They called her Carmel before, something else now, I forget; but she was just Mel when she had this body. Rich kid, lives on the high side somewhere. Fancied being a filly for a season but I think she got bored pretty quickly. Not the cab, you wouldn't catch her cabbing. What I heard, she couldn't face all the eating, so she traded up. The way it works here, if we take on a body we can take the same name but add a number, so everyone knows it's not original to us. I have to be Mel-2 on the record; nobody bothers with it else. This was only hers for a couple of months. Me, I've been pulling a cab with it two years now. Everybody knows. Mel is me and this is what I look like," and she stamped again for emphasis, without for a moment losing the rhythm of her trot.

It was too much for me, I was reeling where I sat. For a little while I watched the traffic, but even the maddest excesses of the parade couldn't distract me now. I dissembled, briefly; said, "I didn't realise you had identity laws, on Rotten Row?"

She snorted back at me. "'Course we do. Too much money, on the high sides; too much opportunity to get at it, from the Downchute. They watch the decants carefully, especially those of us who are second-use or more."

27

There it was again, and I couldn't ignore it. "Second use? Does that really mean what I think it means?"

"You think I could afford a full custom job like this, fresh out of the tank? You have got so much to learn, mister. What do I call you, anyway?"

Half a dozen sharper answers rose in my mind, but all I said was, "My name is duLaine." *And not unknown in my own system and a dozen more besides,* but there was no point saying so here. Rotten Row never looks beyond its own horizon.

Child of my culture, I was the citizen they'd made me, trembling almost under the shock of what she'd said. None of the broadcasts I'd seen, none of my research had thrown this up, that they re-used their discards here. I could understand authority censoring that news, even while it allowed people to come here and discover it for themselves; perhaps I should have talked to more tourists. Perhaps I'd been too proud, too confident of my superior motives and disdainful of theirs. Well, this is why I do what I do: art is an expression of the need, the yearning to learn from others.

And that's why I was here, and oh, I did need to talk to her about this; and oh, I couldn't do it now.

Rotten Row is a major investment of steel and plass and time, it's a long long lap around the length of it. Even so, sitting in the high seat of her cab and looking over her head, I could see the curvature of the road, the station's arc, how it rose upward far ahead. I said, "Mel, could I hire you for the day, tomorrow?"

"'Course. Welcome." A full day's work, no touting for fares, and a fee that she could set herself? I hadn't doubted it. "Where do you want to go?"

"All the way. A full lap."

"In a day?"

"Can't you do that?" I had no idea, it struck me suddenly, about the endurance even of a true horse, let alone an artifi-cial construct, a human/horse hybrid. And she did look more

28

scrawny even than before, seen from this angle, looking down on her jutting bones.

"Not in one day. I'm only human," and her hind leg stamped to underscore the joke of it, and she glanced around to see that happen, just to emphasise the irony.

"How long would it take, then?"

"I could do it in a day and a night and a day—but only on stims, which would cost us both, and you'd only see the road. Better to take it in stages, take your time," hire her for more days, for a week or more. No doubt she understood already that I could afford it.

This was her world, and I was out of my depth in it; that much I understood myself. Also, she looked hungry. And she was living in a second-hand discard, and—

Enough. I said, "Fine. We'll do that. You be my guide as well as my transport, yes?"

"Lovely," she said, beaming back at me. "I'll take you to all my favourite places. Fifty, sixty degrees of arc, that's enough in a day; and we'll sleep somewhere different every night, I like that. Anything particular you want to see, just say. Anything you've heard about, anything I mention. We've got plenty going on here, that they don't tell the tourists. Anyone you want to meet, that too. I know them all."

I was sure of it. Mel was a gift to me, more than she knew, and she was sure enough on her own account. Mel-2: that number, though, that still troubled me deeply. Interested as I was—no, more than that: fascinated, attracted, appalled—it was a relief none the less when she turned forward again and let me just sit and look for a while. Looking is my trade, or the start of my trade, my seedcorn proposition. It's something I do well.

Even when what I'm looking at is so alien it defies any power of my describing, I still do the looking. Don't turn away.

The parade on Rotten Row goes in both directions simultane-ously. Of course it does: the parade is their life for these people, their life becomes the parade. Going out and coming home again, shopping or cruising or visiting friends, they're always on view and always exhibiting. Dressed for it or not, taking their time or in a hurry, even *in extremis*—I saw one boy in tears behind his feathered hands, running as he wept, making distressful sounds through the hidden secret of his mouth, and wondered if he knew Tethys—they can't or don't avoid the main drag, the gravitic drag of the Row proper. Sorrows and joys and the daily grind, all of it is peppered with display. All life is conducted face-up, in the certainty of other people's watching.

Even the rich, who could afford privacy if they wanted it: even they parade themselves, their wealth, their accomplishments—and yes, perhaps their distresses too—down here with the common folk, their lower neighbours and attendant souls.

Even here, there are social strata. Here, as so often elsewhere, they're literal as well as metaphorical. The Row runs as it were at the bottom of a valley, long and straight and unbroken, steeply banked. It's lined with stores and workshops and dealerships on both sides, a broderie of markets. Behind, the walls of the habitat begin to rise, and the internal architecture clings to them: climbing the high sides, they call it here. The higher, as you'd expect, the more expensive. Go high enough—above the chop-houses and open stalls, the rented rooms and stables, above the hostels and the gaming-rooms, above the good hotels and the private houses, into the strata of the seriously wealthy and the phenomenally rich—and there are the people who really don't need to parade. If they chose to, they could keep their morphing for private display, only to each other. They have private roads hung from the height, where the walls curve over to become a roof, a ceiling, a sealing-in to give the orbital station its ovoid section, its integrity and its strength; they have private arrangements, no doubt, to convey themselves to and fro. They needn't ever come down.

Need seems to make no difference. The highsiders still do come down, to show themselves to tourists and the aspirational. They do it with more clamour, and more rarely; they don't scuttle down-Row in a late search for food or prophylactics or a smoke. Nevertheless, down they come, as though there was no point in living here, except to make show of yourself.

There *is* no point in living here, except to make show of yourself. I'm only surprised that so many of them acknowledge it. The impulse to art can be fugitive and hard to recognise, where you thought perhaps you were building a body, or a lifestyle, or a future way to be.

That first day, that first hour on the road I was lucky—perhaps: I thought so at the time—to see one of the great modmeisters on parade. Ignorant as I was, blinded as I was, there was still no space to doubt what was occurring or how significant she was, the one who came.

I heard her, to be fair, before I saw her. Or at least I heard her coming, I heard her announced. Mel was quicker, she knew already; likely she'd been watching the road far ahead, where it curved upward to allow that. Where you could see a significant shift in traffic, a swirl in the kaleidoscope's gaudy, long before any rumour of it reached you otherwise.

Speed of light, speed of sound; speed of thought, speed of action. By the time I heard those distant trumpets, Mel had already started to slip sideways through the traffic, from the centre of the road where she'd been giving me best views of the parade, right in the heart of it, sights and sounds and smells together. By the time I made out the snap of forcewhips giving an irregular staccato back-beat to the trumpeting, we were safely off to one side, just not quite grinding one wheel against the kerb. She was as careful of her cab as she was of her fares; I liked that.

She needed to be careful. Suddenly there were surging bodies all about us. The light frame of the jitney might easily have been overturned in the press, throwing me out and breaking spars and dragging her down with it, if she hadn't been ready to kick out at threats far heavier than she was, to punch and shove when she had to, to curse with a savagery at least as effective as her fists.

Her ferocity in defence of what was hers, her passenger and her livelihood and her place in this small world: it kept us upright and unmolested in that nervous, excited, unpredictable crowd; it kept me fascinated by her, watching her, what little time there was until the roadshow arrived; it kept me in that high and convenient seat, where I could see the roadshow quite unencumbered.

First came the trumpeters—except that no, those were of course not trumpets of any description that were sounding to warn people away and announce the coming of their lady. Any more than those were forcewhips that they snapped to drive the laggardly aside. This was Rotten Row; why would they need tools, instruments, devices?

There were four of them abreast, and between their own selves and the space they created around them, they took up the full width of the highway. They were vast enough in themselves, great broad bipeds barely remembering that they had been human once, that there was man-shape hidden somewhere within those enormities of flesh. Their legs were mammoth, thick and shaggy, crucial to carry the weight of muscle and bone above. Torsos and arms were human-normal, more or less, except for the simple ungodly size of them; heads were—well, something else. Unhuman. It was hard to see past the trunks that made their trumpets: not truly elephantine, but closer to that than anything other, anything I'd seen. The skin, no, hide was purplish-black, ridged and seamed; hugely flexible, those trunks reared up in military order to blast another call ahead, *clear the way!* coupled with *here she comes, all come, all see her come!*

Muscled as they were, artificially boosted under that creased hide, they could have managed a forcewhip in each hand without thinking, but they didn't need to. They had tails that flicked and snapped, living rawhide; and there was something mechanical or biomechanical, grown or surgically added, that threw sparks with every snap. Sparks that stung: people yelped or screamed when they were struck.

None of this was fancy, just for show. When they called to clear the way, they really meant it.

Behind them came their mistress's chariot, drawn by a team of four great centaur-males, harnessed two and two. These again were built on a vast scale, hugely bigger than Mel's slight frame; they stood twice as tall, perhaps, with many times her bulk behind them. Luxuriant blond beards cloaked their naked chests, and the same hair made wild manes all down their backs; their hooves were iron-shod. The harness they wore looked more imperative than Mel's, meant to limit and control. Once strapped in—someone else's task, surely—they'd have small chance of slipping free. Small choice, too, where they drew their burden. There were reins on the equipage and a driver holding them, with a genuine forcewhip in his other hand. While I was watching he cracked it only for effect, but I did wonder.

It looked like a chariot she rode in, at least from the front, gilded and ornate; in truth it was a long wheeled platform, room enough and to spare for her and those who attended her, servants or suppli-cants or junior sisters. I couldn't guess. There was a handful of them, human-normal in size and approximation, clad in simple colours to complement or contradict the colours in their skin and hair. One was scaled, I thought, as soft and iridescent as a dustsnake.

Their mistress kept outlandish heralds, perhaps for contrast; she kept her attendants decorative but neutral, unoriginal, unchallenging. Perhaps for emphasis, or just not to distract, not to lessen her own impact.

She needn't have worried, if worry she did. I had seen things, extraordinary things, on the Row already; she was in a different class. Another order of magnitude, and of achievement.

There are hierarchies of body-sculpture, inevitably: hierarchies of time and wealth and imagination. I knew all of that already, I'd seen the broadcasts, both uncut and in Awful Warning format.

That's just data, though. This was something utterly other: experi-ence, actuality, the reason I came.

She lay sprawled on her chariot, on her stage like a giant, like a work of art made manifest, fallen live out of an ancient painting: half again as tall as any of her attendants, four or five times the bulk of them, vast and fleshy and seemingly unaltered else from human basecode. Naked and enormous, she lay there on a slab of rock with her hair tossed wild around her. Chains on her wrists and ankles held her fast to bolts in the rock, and she watched the sky in a dreadful anticipation.

So did I, then, and I do believe I was looking for a dragon.

No such came. There wasn't really sky to search in any case, only the high curvature of steel lined with plass, the roof of the world, the ceiling of this autophagic tube, this torus of their exile. A light-bar burned all around its length, a measure of its circumference; later that would dim to a twilight and then to full dark, because of course they liked their night parades, how not? There would be no reason else to schedule night and noon in an orbital like this, but there was no reason else for Rotten Row to be here; it was all about the parade. And augmented or otherwise, humans respond differently in the dark. We're wired that way.

Or rewired, here. No doubt there were nocturnal creatures on the station, made for night. Eyes that would burn in this light, skin that would crack and dry. There must also be parties, reputations that would be lost in light; of a certainty, Rotten Row would have its colony of vampires. With, no doubt, its entourage of victims, *feed on me*. No matter how they played with bodies, the poor would be always with them, pleading for a subservient space.

Like this woman's attendants, her centaurs, her heralds. Playing petty parts in her tableau, living in what shapes, what morphs she decreed and bonded to her for the privilege, because they could never afford such bodies on their own account. I was guessing, yes, but doing it credibly, persuading myself. That would be the alternative to Mel's freelance hustling: to sell themselves to a wealthy patron, play someone else's games and wear their prescribed bodies like a uniform supplied. For some, that would be compensation enough.

It wasn't my place, but I was proud of Mel for resisting that, for taking the other way: working for herself and wearing what body she could afford, even if it had been worn before. Even if that thought did still make my belly twist.

Like the woman on the rock, I looked up high for one more player in this drama; like her I saw it come, cruciform against the cool blaze of the light-bar, breaking that endless line of glare.

Breaking it, looming, swooping down. Casting a shadow first across the whole performance, then specifically over her.

Swooping down and striking, hard and deep.

Not a dragon, no. This was a bird, or as far that way as she cared to have him flung: still with the memory of human about him, but remade enough to make Tethys envious. Wings and claws and beak he had, and all of them practical, effective. Dark and gleaming feathers and no clothes else, no attempt to hide his bare and human chest. Still a mammal, then, or at least he still had nipples. That might not matter to the gene-sculptors, but it might to the biophysics of the 'chute. I didn't know, either way: whether grafting avian characteristics onto a mammalian base added to the complications, whether the mechanisms of transfer demanded a measurably human core. Aliens don't use 'chutes: whether for reasons of politics or science, I simply didn't know. If it became important, I could learn. What seemed more important now was the fact that I didn't know, that the paranoia of my own culture was enough to keep even the Upshot ignorant of what could or couldn't be done with our own defining technology.

These are the doubts, the questions, the revelations that art is made from. It is itself a grafting, emotion onto matter, insight rendered in another form. No wonder that the Upshot do not care for it; it brushes against their most sensitive boundaries, and that itself is an insight that informs my art. We work in circles, always, talking about the way we talk and listening to ourselves, learning from what we say.

Learning from what we see. I saw this bird-man, this elaborated eagle plunge and strike, his talons digging into the woman's belly, ripping her open.

I saw his beak dip and tear; I saw it come up with gobbets of dark wet matter that he swallowed bird-wise, throwing his head back and letting gravity tug them down his feathered throat.

I saw her suffer, writhing in her chains, with never a sound escaping her proud lips.

I saw her maidens cower, inadequate and helpless, picked or trained for that.

I saw that everyone was watching, because this was after all the parade, this was what they were here for, either to watch it or to be a part of it and either way it was their responsibility to give it due attention. Besides, where else would you look, when all of this was happening right there in the road?

I saw that only the tourists were enthralled, appalled, capturing it all for absent friends. The residents, the modified watched with a critical gaze, as though they'd seen it all before.

I was fairly sure about that already, but I'd still ask Mel after it was over.

In the meantime, it went on. The eagle ate her liver, while she bled and bled without ever quite bleeding out. Pale and magnificent, she lay and laboured for breath, for life, as she should. And meantime her centaurs dragged her forward, and her heralds announced her coming; and caught where we were in the traffic, crushed to the side of the road, there was only so much of her that I could see. Even standing in the jitney, craning over the roof. She still moved inexorably out of my view.

When at last the bird-man heaved himself into the air again, belly-full and struggling, I saw that. He must have left her with an aching void in her abdomen, but I couldn't see that. Her maidens clustered around her and I did see that, distantly, the movement of slender girls about a giant form. What they did, what resulted, all of that was lost in distance and the sudden hubbub in her wake, the business of the road reawakened, Mel too pulling out and moving on, a terminus to my staring.

I said, "What, then, what now? Do they take her to the 'chute and just discard that body, quick, before she dies of it . . . ?" Extreme wealth can be extremely wasteful, flauntingly so. I'd met people who would be amused by such profligacy, especially in the faces of their hungry servants. Others who would see it as reinforcement, *this is why you serve me, because I can do this and you not.*

Art too can be wasteful, in pursuit of a statement. I have known artists who would do exactly the same, for exactly the opposite reason: to say, *this is what you serve, and why you should not.*

Glancing back, she let me see her smile. "Who, Promethea? Not her. That body's self-repairing. And nerveless where it matters, no suffering into truth for her. She's got a reservoir of fresh blood right there in the cart, and nurses to watch over her; they'll whisk her off now upsides to one of her rich friends, and she'll recover in luxury, grow it all back and do it all again. She's doing this once in every twelve degrees of arc, it's her project."

The woman Promethea clearly thought she was making art. I thought she was probably mistaken. I thought she confused display with meaning, enactment with interpretation. Even so, I did suddenly want to talk to her about it.

I said, "So what happens then, once she's gone full circle and given her performance in every segment?"

"Then she'll ditch that body—not pass it on, she wouldn't want it still around to stage second-rate imitations or worse, put to other uses—and move on to something new. She'll have it all planned out already, body in the tank, the other actors bought and rehearsed and ready."

"And, what, she'll change her name to suit the new role?"

"Yes, of course. The name goes with the body," and the question didn't even seem worth asking, not to Mel, whose name had likewise come with the body, who would clearly think nothing of changing name with every decant. It was another slap in the face to the ID laws I knew, all the codes I came from. Another reason for Rotten Row's isolation here, its exclusion from the Upshot network. If you can change your name and make your body over as you will, how could anyone be certain of you, ever? How could you even be certain of yourself?

Art trades on uncertainty, but banks and governments do not.

"What about the eagle, must he change too, to suit her?"

Mel shrugged, an oddly small gesture against her pony bulk. "I suppose. If he wants to stay in her service. He might be happy with what he's got, and want to keep it—but I don't know how he's going to eat, without her. I doubt he can talk, even, with that beak; he's been made over too far. And he's got no hands to write with, to tell people what he wants. I suppose he could use a keypad, but even that would be hard. In that state, I'd say she owns him, absolutely. Hell, if she decided not to change him, to keep him as a pet, how would he complain?"

To whom? might be another question. I understood the shape of social hierarchy here, it followed money, as everywhere; I had yet to learn the hierarchies of power. She was right, though, the eagle was mute of morph, almost without recourse and mortgaged to his mistress. His own choices—or his needs, perhaps, his desperate craving—had indentured him beyond hope of release, left him hostage entirely to her will.

I shuddered, and thought him stupid. And then thought how much his mistress would hate it, that I had seen her performance and spent my time since considering her servant instead of her. And felt better, a little, and turned my attention back to the life of the road around us and this day's end and the next to come.

Looking forward, I couldn't help but look at Mel as she worked, as she gripped the shafts of her cab and pulled it, me, at a steady clip. The jitney's weight and mine and all my bags', all that was taken by her horse-body through the harness that she wore. She gripped the shafts for comfort or control or some illusion of it, nothing more; her arms weren't towing, there was no work going through her shoulders. None the less she sweated, above and below her breastband, as her chestnut coat lathered up. It was a reminder, I guess, that she wasn't two separate creatures, human-head and horse-body, that worked individually and could be considered apart.

That started me wondering, technical questions: how could she get breath enough to oxygenate all that flesh and bone that hauled me? She must have way more blood in her body than two human-normal lungs could feed, and she ought to be in debt past all recovery. I could hear her breathing, as I could see her sweat: working but not labouring, I thought, still on the right side of efficient.

How much she needed to eat to fuel that body, that again was a question. I thought she wasn't getting enough, from the look of her: scrawny in her human half—though young women often are—and bone-bare as a pony. That was the giveaway, because horses like to be fat.

Also, she'd said that the other young woman, the one who'd had this same body before her—

—though I still shuddered, wanted to pull away entirely from that thought and all that it implied, criminal heresy in my head and I wanted shot of it quick, before it made its way into my art—

—she'd said the first Mel "couldn't face all the eating." I wondered what she'd had to eat, and how much of it, and if Mel-2 had the same difficulty or else just couldn't afford the quantities. Hungry from choice, hungry from revulsion or simply from lack of means: one or another of those, I was sure. She was hungry, and I felt guilty to sit in her cab and make her work. The fact that I was her meal ticket—today, tomorrow, several days to come—was a consolation, but a small one. Inadequate.

She pulled and I watched the parade some, more the slow flow of shifting scenery. At this level it was all much of a muchness, shabby workshops and markets with the inevitable allure of cheap exoticism. I'm not immune, though I am perhaps case-hardened. Wherever humankind goes, it takes poverty and hunger with it. Hierarchies happen, whether they're imported as is or recreated in situ. Wealth and opportunity lift some above the throng, leave the rest to improvise whatever substitutes they can find for money or authority or luck. The resourceful have their charms; societies create whole strata of resource.

But those at the bottom tend to walk around with their heads tilted back, gazing up at what they lack, what they most desire, elevation. Here, that was not a metaphor. I did the same thing, letting my eyes rise to the heights, passing over layers of increasingly sophisticated build until high walls and privacy refused me. No matter: I wasn't looking to ogle the rich in their fastnesses. I'm a climber, in any discard and on any world. I was looking for pitches, scrambles, possibilities.

Looking and not really seeing anything I could use. I've climbed on orbitals before, an interesting structure can be as rewarding as a cliff-face or as challenging—in one or two cases, simply as big—as a mountain. Rotten Row was different: too stratified, perhaps. At any rate there were too many breaks in its ascendancy, too many lanes and private roads criss-crossing where it climbed. It offered nothing sheer, nothing to engage with.

Mostly, then, I watched Mel. Sitting this close, above and behind, I was fascinated by the workings of her body and intrigued by the mysteries of her life, intrigued too by my own mix of fascination and repugnance. I was working now, as much as she was: this is where art happens, in that encounter-space between what's new and what's established, what I bring and what I find.

When she drew to a stop, my disappointment wasn't for loss of the tour, the views I was allegedly paying her to show me. It was for loss of movement in her, the play of muscle and bone, the shift of light on sweat on shifting skin.

She turned, and pushed a hand through sticky hair—and that in itself was startling, so human a gesture after I had been so long absorbed in what was most animal about her—and said, "I need to rest, to eat. I guess I could keep going until lights-out, but there's a good flophouse just here—well, the stables are good, and I hear good things about the bedrooms—so what say we call this a day? We've only done fifteen degrees of arc, but we can make up distance another day, get an early start and really hammer the road. The night scene's good round here, too. I can show you some of that, if you'd like it."

"Of course I would. That's what I'm here for, as much as this," with a gesture at the cab, the road, the long parade. "I want to see everything there is to see. Whatever's feasible." If it meant more time with Mel, that was ideal; I wanted to see her, in her world, living her life. Outside the shafts of her cab. With me in tow it would be a distorted picture, she'd still be acting as guide, but you lose what restraints you can and live with whatever's left. "And I'd be glad if you'd eat with me, let me buy you dinner . . ."

She snorted, for a moment all horse. I wondered how much the body did influence the character. Every new discard affects us, inevitably. We change, we grow into and out of our bodies. The very young sometimes have male and female selves, depending on the gender of their current discard; we learn to integrate, but there is always influence. Hormonal, cultural, otherwise.

She said, "Sorry, but you really don't know what you're saying."

"Well, no. I'm new here. I had wondered what you need to eat—vegetarian, I'm assuming, unless there's some radical re-engineering in your gut. But not hay, I'm assuming that also . . . ?"

"Vegetarian, yes, of course; and no, not hay; but—oh, come down to the stables once you're settled and I'll show you. And then you'll know, not to offer to buy a girl dinner on Rotten Row."

And she grinned, and clicked herself into a trot again, and took us off the Row.

There are lanes and tracks and wider ways branching off from either side all the way around. Some are local, access to the shops and stalls and alleys, the accommodation behind and above; some are more ambitious, proper roads with broken backs, switching steeply left and right as they struggle to make the height of the upper echelons. The wealthy may have more elegant, less frantic ways to go home, but if so they keep them private.

This was an unprepossessing lane she took me up, squeezed between the windowless wall of a godown and a shack handbuilt from recycled panels, where a man behind a hatch sold greasy twists of something I couldn't identify by sight or smell, that he didn't bother to identify with signage. Presumably his customers would know and the rest of us didn't need to. There was a sign on the godown wall, pointing towards "Ro's Livery". If I had been alone, if I had even understood it to be a hostel, I wouldn't have given a moment's thought to asking for a bed there.

This is why we look for guides, why I can't work without one. How else would I know where to look, what to look at? If I find myself on a high place and set apart, it's because I found someone to lead me there.

Mel brought me to Ro's Livery, pulling up in front of a door that looked to be salvaged from somewhere else entirely, transparent plass showing its weary age in the decals that had been inadequately scraped away. It wasn't only bodies that they reused here.

But the door was sparkling-clean, and so was the hall beyond it; and a lad came tumbling out to take my bags, human-normal as far as I could tell from looking. Perhaps they didn't practise engineering on their children, in the womb or afterward. Mel was waiting, hot and tired and dirty; she needed me to move. So I climbed down and watched her clop along to a broad and open gate that presumably led into the stable yard. I wondered if that was a problem for her human half, that she had to be housed like an animal.

The boy took me inside, and there was Ro: not the fat and flustered landlord of tradition, kind and overworked and heavy-handed, but a lean and weary sophisticate who seemed far out of keeping with his slightly tawdry location, even before I took his second head into account.

They were, quite definitely, a first and a second head: the one dominant and dealing with the world, the other inward-looking, downcast, muttering figures under his breath. I supposed that must be useful, when you ran a business. If you didn't have the tech, or access to a hi-hal to run your numbers for you.

I wondered how on earth they'd worked it, at the 'chute: did two people go in for the upfling, and only one come out the other end? Or had Ro's single personality been somehow divided—just a string of ones and zeroes, after all, you could do any arithmetic you liked with that—and distributed between two waiting brains?

Perhaps he'd had multiple personalities to start with, and this was a medical intervention.

And how long would it be, before I had been here long enough to ask . . . ?

For now, there were other and immediate questions. A room, a bed? Of course, no problem. And my cabbie in the stables? Yes, indeed. The boy Dolph would see to her comfort and valet the rickshaw too, and her bill was mine, understood, absolutely— Oh, it's *Mel?* Mel-2? That's a different matter entirely. No, Dolph, not that key; take the gentleman to the top floor, best view of the Row and most welcome. If I still wanted to claim Mel's bill, I'd have to fight Ro for it; she was a friend of the house and always welcome, a guest by any measure, and if that cab wasn't gleaming before we moved on tomorrow poor Dolph would learn all about it, in a lesson taught by bruises . . .

My own room turned out to be a suite, then; and if it was still a suite in a shabby hostel, almost the flophouse that Mel had named it, it was clean and comfortable and the water was hot. And the view, as promised, was splendid. It was starting to darken out there—what my primitive planet-natural mind still wanted to call dusk or even sunset—and there was a corresponding shine to the streets and alleys that lined the Row, as their bright inducements beckoned tourists and residents alike.

The parade itself had dwindled, perhaps, but certainly not died. Some modifications brought their own light with them, and would likely not come out before this, for fear that no one would see how their veins or their eyes glowed, how colours ran like lights beneath their skin. Others had remade themselves for shadow, and slipped now along the quiet Row like the whisper of a threat, gifting the circuit a darker self, an inverse flipside show.

Even so, the main business of the night was off the thoroughfare. Street-stalls and comfort-houses, drugs and drinks and smokes and food. If it was still all about display, it was on a local level now, one to one and you'd really need to be there.

I was hungry myself and for more than eating, for the entirety of the world I saw out there, the denizens in close-up. I ached to be among them, but first thoughts of food reminded me of Mel. I had promised to visit her in the stables, another kind of close-up: no display, or at least none that was public.

Down the stairs, then, down all the stairs, because engineering is expensive and muscles are cheap. More work than I liked, in a body not yet ready for it. Bodies in the tank have their exercise electrically; they come out fit for display purposes, but utterly unused to actual movement under gravity. It takes a little time to get them habituated.

There had to be a back door from the hostel to the stable yard, but it wasn't obvious from the hallway. There was a door into the kitchens, a door into the bar, a corridor that might lead anywhere. Other doors were closed and unforthcoming. Ro was busy, head to head to head with a labourer or perhaps a tradesman, a supplier of something. A denizen. The broad bull shoulders told me that, and the lashing tail suggested that he wasn't happy. Not a conversation to interrupt.

There was no sign of the boy Dolph, so I was thinking to slip out of the front door and down the alley, to the yard gate and find Mel that way; but Ro caught sight of me across the bull-man's shoulder.

"duLaine?"

The name brought the bull head swinging around on its great neck. I was aware of vast bovine eyes in a white-furred face that still had some trick of the human to it despite its breadth and weight, despite the wet purple snout, despite the ring—the ring!—through the nostrils there, despite the cloud of warm wet grassy breath that enveloped me from too close, far too close.

"You are duLaine?" Words were hard for him, with a tongue and jaw not shaped for shaping sound; they came out thick and slurred. Which he knew, to judge by the temper of his tail.

I bowed my head, striving to be nothing but civil, to give him nothing at all to work against. "I am."

"My master has heard that you were here. An artist. Another artist, yes. He sends for you. Me, he sends me . . ."

It was clearly not an invitation to refuse. I could make one guess already, who had sent it. Which was ideal for me, if true; but, "Wait," I said, "your master has heard of my work?"

He shrugged, as massive a gesture in him as it was petite in Mel. I thought it highly unlikely that immersion protocols or even word of them had reached this far. On the other hand, I thought it highly likely that a young man in need of money or patronage or both—a young man employed at the 'chute, say, a young man with expensive ambitions, wings in his eyes—might let word slip out of my own arrival, *an artist passing through, yes, and I can guess exactly where he'll be tonight . . .*

Fine, let that go; I was in no position to resent it. Even so, "I have promised my company to a lady tonight." That was a formal protest, no more, pitched for Ro's ears and attention.

As expected, the bull just shrugged it off. Ro said, "Please, don't concern yourself with Mel-2. Dolph and I will see her happy tonight. If we need to. She has more friends in this arc than she has flies in high summer."

I did not believe for a moment that the Terminus ran to either summer or flies, or that Mel would endure the latter if it did. The rest, I took on trust.

And still repined, would still far have preferred to pass this first night in her bright company. But there was no choice being offered to me here, and art seldom works to our convenience or pleasure. I nodded my thanks, left my profound apologies with promises for tomorrow, and followed the bull-man out into the street.

He had to sidle through the door, and still his shoulders barely fitted in the frame. His arms were awkward, over-muscled, long; his legs were brutal and barefoot, bare-hooved. He wore a loose shirt and trousers, as crudely made as the body they made to shroud.

It was no surprise to find another carriage in the alley outside. In blunt contrast to Mel's light jitney, this was a heavy square construction, all mass and effort even in its emptiness. I climbed in reluctantly, consoling myself—vaguely—that I would be adding little to the bull's workload, a bare fraction of his burden's weight.

There was a yoke of leather and chain that lay across his shoulders, that lifted the poles into his grasp. No harness else, no way to distribute the load. He heaved and hauled. I could see great muscles shift, straining his clothes as iron-rimmed tyres began to roll. I sat on a padded bench, but not much padded; there were as few compromises made for my comfort as for his.

He took me back along the Row, the way we'd come, though not so far: back and then up, up and up. Here on this switchback climb the plass was corrugated, to give better grip to him and his kind; if

46

it gave me a rougher, jolting ride, no matter. The road was a workers' way, not laid for my benefit or any passenger's.

Not mattering, then—so very obviously not mattering—I did wonder quite why I had been sent for, quite so imperatively. The immediacy didn't seem to fit. I was used to being either fêted or ignored, depending how close I was to my home system; this was uncomfortably neither the one thing nor the other, neither a welcome to the acclaimed duLaine nor a blank shrug for the unknown. I felt summoned like a craftsman, like an artisan to be interrogated for a job of work. Fetched, but not in comfort; fetched but not escorted, not companioned, left to the dubious care of the haulier because I was worth no more.

Or not known to be worth more, that at least. I was being given an opportunity, perhaps, to justify myself. I might have taken insult, but there really was no point. No one knew me here; they had only my own valuation to go by, that I was an artist at all.

Besides, this was all material to work with. How people react to my art—and to me—yields up an aspect of the art itself. How not? The deeper I sink into them, the deeper I find myself sunken. That is inherent. The one element I cannot outreach is my own self, reaching.

Up on the high road, slung beneath the ceiling, the ride was smooth and easy again, iron tyres grumbling in an undertone but finding never a catch or a crack to complain at, never a flaw. If Tethys had ever been this high, he must have trodden softly, not to scratch the plass.

Up here, houses clung to the vertical sidewalls of the habitat or else hung as the road did from above; gardens were all galleries, as artificial as their owners. I gazed and gazed, and swallowed drugs and wished that it was Mel who drew me here. It ought not to matter, it is perhaps a flaw in me that reflects itself in my work, but I do form quick attachments. And I do prefer to meet a new environment through a single perspective, mediated by an individual. With good reason. I had seen the parade below with Mel's lively commentary attached: her body as eloquent as her tongue, bespeaking passion and engagement, delight and fascination and contempt in unequal measure, unpredictably. All of that I could work with.

Here I was getting nothing from the bull-man, though we were passing wonders: no conversation, no reactions. He ran toilingly, head down, closed in. And yes, of course I could work with that—but it would bring a wholly different palette to the work, another mood, almost another piece entirely. And yes, I could marry the two, of course I could; I could be my own linking-matter if need be, the only constant, the alien view.

But oh, I would have preferred Mel and her instincts, her insights to govern mine.

Up here, what would have been a private driveway on land became a bridge between the flying road and the clinging house. Awful space hung below us, a dreadful fall; and no, of course the bridge did not shake beneath the bull's pounding hooves and the rumble of the heavy carriage, but I shook anyway.

And wondered, if a man fell from the height—if his carriage skidded, say, or the bull that pulled it because there was no gripping on the ice-slick plass up here, and they all tumbled together through those obviously frail railings and so fell, carriage and bull and man all three—whether there would be time enough to cancel the orbital's spin, let the gravity decay, let us not fall after all.

And decided that there wouldn't, of course not, no; and mocked myself for the fancy even as I did for the fear that underlay it. Climbers make bad passengers, that's traditional. We trust our own hands above anyone's else, we all want to lead on the rope, but I'm an extreme case even in that phobic fraternity. The fall is always in my eyes and I hate, I *hate* to cede control.

Which is why, one reason why I swallow so many drugs. Here they were no help, because the bull-man gave me nothing, not so much as his name. I could have sailed over that gap on Mel's projected confidence, but she was left below, beneath us here. I swallowed drugs in any case, wearing down my own walls in hopes of breach to come, and tried not to look out or down, not to imagine. It was always better to look upward at a climb, feet planted on the solid at its foot. And then to send it, all bone and muscle and mind working with the rock, an act of engagement, like the making of art; and then to walk away. And not look back, certainly not ever to look down. I hated downclimbing. I'd always rope or jump or take a lift, any way plausible or possible away from a peak, sooner than go back the way I'd come, all reach and cling.

Across the bridge, then, safe of course; and through a gate into a courtyard where it was almost—almost!—possible to forget the drop below, invisible beneath this floor of mock-stone plass.

Or else I could concentrate on the drop and almost, almost manage to overlook the insult as I was borne across the courtyard and around the side of the house to another yard entirely, where the staff were stabled.

No doubt other, more delicate servants slept in regular rooms beneath their patron's roof. Perhaps some of those stabled here were not morphs at all but legitimate animals, kept as pets or beasts of fancy burden. But certainly the bull-man's stall was here; I could feel that in him, something at last, a craving for ease, an end of work, perhaps the hope of rut.

Perhaps I would have felt all that, gathered it all without the drugs at all. Certainly the man who stepped out of the staff door now, who came down the steps to greet me there in the yard, his lip curled at the steaming bull-man in his sweat-soaked clothes, and I thought he saw it all himself without benefit of drugs.

"Very well, Bulgar. Eat, drink, get yourself cleaned up," *do as you will* his hands said, in little gestures of dismissal. And then he turned to me and his smile was all apology, a steward on behalf of his patron, "I'm afraid your ride was rougher than it should have been, Master duLaine, in every respect," with a rueful glance at the carriage as the bull unhitched himself. "My master would brook no delay, though. As soon as he heard that you were here, he was determined that you should come. Art has no patience, we learn to say in this household; it will not wait on the world."

That was not my experience, and not my art. But he said it almost as another kind of apology, as though he were almost apologising for his patron this time. He was a clever man, this one, who walked on cat's-paws and carried his tail high, though he seemed human-normal above the waist. I wondered if there were whiskers in his future, and whether it might be polite to ask.

"Besides," he went on in the face of my silence, "we have another guest tonight, our own Promethea. Of course my master would wish to bring the two of you together, to hear art converse with art . . ."

Yes, of course. I had half-expected that.

Balance and fine motor control may take a little time to acquire, in a new discard; expressions are always hard, so that we goon and grimace for a day or two, overstating emotions, smiling too widely and scowling when we mean to frown; a blank face, though, I can always be sure of. Almost always. True shock will cut through even my control, and Rotten Row had offered shocks already, but that was rare. We tend to cultivate neutrality anyway, we Upshot, exactly to stop ourselves gawping like mock-humans as we come out of the 'chute and into another world and another and another. For me, in my work, it was essential.

In my life too it was frequently useful. As now, under the steward's gaze, I was as unyielding as plass, as unforthcoming as the best of diplomats. *Take what you can, take everything you can; give nothing away of yourself.* It was the rule I lived and worked by, and what the drugs were intended to achieve: to open me up, to make my borders permeable but in the one direction only, incoming.

He led me into the house, and swiftly—apologetically, perhaps—through bare bleak corridors, servants' ways to a pass door into another world. Yet another. For somewhere so small and self-contained, Rotten Row harboured a startling range of extremes crowded startlingly close together. Necessarily so, I supposed, it was in the nature of the place, but it was still one more factor to deal with. To factor in.

Behind me, naked undecorated plass, work unsoftened, unadorned. Around and ahead of me now, luxury beyond anything I'd seen yet in this habitat or most others. In my home system I am famous, wealthy on my own account and welcome in the houses of the wealthiest. That becomes less and less true, the further I travel. I had never come this far before; the abrupt contrast might have had a measure of influence. Even so, this was astonishing.

And savage, almost violent in its assertions; and clumsy, almost vulgar in its effects. The work of a vulgar mind, I thought, only that the work itself rose above its own source under the impulse of its own achievement.

I was meant, perhaps, to feel that I had stepped into a private gallery, into the mind of a collector, an aesthete. *I may make nothing of my own,* he wanted to say to me, *but art can also lie in juxtaposition; in bringing these things together, in setting them side by side, I can tell you something of myself.*

Which was true, of course and always; only he wanted me to be impressed by something more than the size of his purse. He showed me the proud contents of his mind, and it appalled me.

We stood in a hallway, nowhere grand, not a destination in itself: and the rug beneath my feet was bright *tophar*-silk, unmistakable, all but unaffordable even on its own planet. And like anything material, of course, incapable of transit through a 'chute. The cost of bringing it this far, the price of transport between the stars was, well, astronomical.

And the rug that hung on the wall beside in brute echo of what lay underfoot, that was old-Earth ancient, worn almost to its base-threads but still a wonder of pattern and craft, of mind and hand together. Bokhara silk and *tophar*-silk—which was of course not silk at all but a mineral construction, an expression of silicon—had nothing to say to each other. Bright plain blocks and faded intricacy, each in its own terms was magnificent, but all they could do was steal light and attention from each other, like children snatching back and forth.

And on a pedestal beside—no, not a pedestal, a gaming-table from Far Col with its inlaid board covered by a square of delicate textured weaving that perhaps I should have sourced at a glance but no one can know it all—was a bold brass head beneath a clear plass dome. It was composed, constructed of cogs and wheels and cables, plugs and studs, the seeming nuts and bolts of bygone days, and again it spoke of old-Earth, though it had never come so far. I knew the woman who made these, a downsider a dozen flings from here; I'd visited her once, to watch her cutting cogs and drawing wires in careful handmade forgery of what was once industrial and common-place. She might have collected the things she used, as others did and do, but it was important to her that they be new, sharp to the eye and to the touch, not complicated by a former use. Her art spoke to the past, not recycled it.

It spoke to me, in these bright mechanical faces that she made and sent out into the inhabited worlds, in slow pursuit of those of us who went ahead by other means.

Here, though? Here were three, no, five works of human hand if I counted in the textile and the table, each one a masterpiece, each staring at the others in mute hostility, reduced by their company where they should have been in glittering and provocative conversation. This wasn't a gallery, it was a storehouse: a disordered appropriation of things, incoherent, useless, harmful. The opposite of art.

It was an abuse, and it made me angry.

Which I concealed—I hoped—as thoroughly as I could as we walked on, over and between and beneath more treasures, more and more, not a collection so much as a bare and greedy accumulation. I thought I could trust my face, not to give me away; I was sure I could trust this discard, because body language is almost the last physical expression to come back. Fresh out of the tank, it was as much as this body could manage to walk in a straightish line with my hands harmlessly behind my back and my head turning to look, turning and turning, saying less even than the pieces I was looking at.

With the face and the body muted, that left only my tongue to curb; and I am a practised and practical diplomat, as any artist must be in pursuit of patronage or data, fees or materials, recognition or workspace or inspiration. We all batten on others, all the time.

Sometimes, we find someone all too willing to be battened upon. This man, my host tonight: I had him fixed and labelled before ever I caught sight of him, before I learned his name.

His steward brought me through a high, high door into a chamber that was higher yet, that tried to impress by scale even before any of the arts and comforts had their chance.

Resolutely unimpressed, I kept my attention rigidly on the people waiting for me: the one rising to his feet in greeting, the other absolutely not.

She too, of course, wanted to impress by scale, the simple dreadful size of her, but I was still resolute.

I have been called stubborn, in my time. There may be some justice in that. It may be a fault; it may be a necessary qualification for what I do, the life I lead, the work I make. It may be an artefact I use.

"Domo Firensay," the man said, coming towards me over all the carpeted expanses of the floor, arms outstretched. "And you are the famous duLaine! Welcome to my house!"

One thing was certain, that I was not famous here. His enthusiasm was as notional, as ignorant as his eye. If he knew anything at all about my work, he had gleaned it this last hour or two, from whatever data banks his wealth could access. Which meant, of course, that he knew nothing. Any immersive practice demands physical interaction, audience with artefact. Full-immer is only more demanding, utterly unforgiving of any compromise.

It was possible that somewhere on his journey here, he might have encountered a piece of mine; but even human space is vast, both broad and dense. The odds were as much against him as his manner was, as his whole house was. Everything here spoke to his dishonesty.

Perhaps I was unfair. Perhaps I only wanted to despise him because of what he'd cost me. Lost potential: the thought of Mel below me and without me was a constant pang, a yearning that I must constantly discount.

Perhaps so, then. Even so, he made it easy. Even now, his hands in mine, his smile, his voice stumbling over its own enthusiasm: he deserved no more credence than I gave him, which was none at all.

Also, he stood shorter than I did and was tubby, balding a little, without a hint of any modification that I could see. Granted that his soft loose clothing might hide a multitude of subtle alterations, but nothing in the man or his house could speak to any subtlety at all. I thought likely this was the same human-normal body he had arrived to, likely years and years before. I thought he had come here to watch and not participate, not to change himself any more than he did the habitat: a permanent tourist, an observer, uninvolved.

Trying to make himself as important as he tried to make his house.

Contempt is an easy one to swallow. I've been doing it all my life.

I bowed over his hands, the perfect hypocrite; and spoke a few soft words of gratitude, all artifice, all learned; and lifted my head towards his gross companion.

Promethea lay on a long daybed, built to her scale, sturdy almost to the point of deformity even where it tried for elegance. She wasn't quite sprawled, not quite lounging, her wound wouldn't quite allow that; no doubt she felt no pain, but the damage was so great that even wealth and design together could not quite bring her to comfort quite so soon.

The wound itself was markedly on display, beneath transparent dressings. Of course it was. By her own choice and his, here she would be one work of art among many.

Diplomacy only goes so far. In me, practised as I am, that would be seldom far enough. I have learned to try, to ape it; I have learned to fail, to expect it, to see my own gauche nature breaking through sooner or later.

Sooner, it would have been that night, except that they expected it too, wanted it and worked for it. An artwork should be looked at, after all.

I was, of course, staring at the wound: too long, too pointedly.

It was, of course, exactly what they wanted.

I realised the one thing and then the other, with time for just a drawing-back between, first hint of an awkward apology.

"No, no," Firensay said; and,

"Please," said Promethea, with an invitation in her gesturing hand, *come closer, look all you desire.*

I did that, then, peering into the great dark ripped hole where her liver ought to be, seeing how the self-repair had already begun, tissue knitting over tear. We can't be sentimental about bodies, any more than we can be shy, those of us who wear them and use them and discard them, time and again; but even so I was uncomfortable, unused to thinking quite so mechanistically. I thought of a human consciousness in an android body, watching it rebuild itself, one component after another. I was a product of my own time, my own society, and too much so perhaps. I was sickened, as I had expected to be: finding exactly what I was looking for.

And swallowed it down, of course, and looked up at her massive face, her massive self-content, and yearned to puncture that. One of those. A fist in the eye was a temptation, but she would never understand it. And would swat me aside with one casual swing of a gigantic arm, injured or not. And would see that as a victory, reinforcement, size as power as justification.

Not that, then. I sighed inside, and readied myself for a wasted evening. There was nothing here I could use, drugs or no drugs. If I tried to make art from this encounter it would be sour and infected, corrupt from its initiation. My own fault, but I couldn't be clear-headed in such a context, I couldn't speak to their values where my own seethed with contempt.

I pined for Mel in her more naive complexity, who was so much what I had come to seek, where these people so very much were not; and dragged out an awkward leering smile for Promethea regardless, playing the diplomat as much as I could still manage.

And said, "There is no pain?"

"No, no," she boomed, her voice in scale with her body, manifest destiny written all through it, "none at all," as though I should be as impressed as she was with the technology of her construct, as though nothing more could matter. As though pain was for the little people.

"You don't feel that pain ought perhaps to be an element in the performance, that Prometheus' suffering is after all the point, and should be registered . . . ?"

The needle question, poisoned with assumptions and pricking, pricking beneath her skin.

"No," she said again, less forcefully, suddenly less certain, "a visual representation only . . ."

"A painting," Firensay said, "brought to life, enacted . . ."

"Ah yes," I murmured, "painting," as though it were a forgotten art, negligible, superseded.

Prick, prick. All evening, with the pricking. My art, my task, my skill derives entirely from the ability to reach beneath another person's skin and teach them another way to feel.

Before this, I had never used it as a weapon.

"Promethea. I've been thinking recently about the transience of grace, or as one might say the grace of transience. The meteor, as against the statue: art that can only be experienced by those who are there, in the moment. How would you square that with your own, ah, habit of repetition, of regular performances, doing the same thing again and again? I would worry, I think, about being neither the meteor nor the statue but falling between the two . . ."

Prick, prick.

"And then this, of course, the restitution: do you feel that an artist, a true artist should always recover so completely from their work, remain unchanged by it, come back just as before . . . ?"

Prick, prick.

In myself I can be gauche and awkward, difficult, I know. In my work I am insidious, and that night I was working. The grace of transience, indeed: I was making a piece that existed only in the air between the three of us, and one of those was blind to it. This was for Promethea alone, to let her finally see herself through someone else's eyes.

Domo Firensay saw none of that. He was only delighted, to have two artists—two renowned artists, he cried, uncorking a bottle for punctuation—in his house and discussing art. Added to his collection, I thought we were, and wondered if he had cameras recording us for proof, for a souvenir, something he could label and exhibit.

The bottle in his hands might as well have been a part of his collection. In fact, it might well have been. We were drinking the rarest of brandies, the true Apollonian; that made me shiver, made me pause, could almost have made me regret my abuse of his hospitality.

Almost.

Instead I abused his generosity also, and drank my share of the bottle. Promethea should have had an appetite to match her size, but in fact she sipped only mechanically, only when she remembered. Which was mostly when I sang the brandy's praise to its provider, poor recompense for the use I was making of him but he seemed pleased enough. Indeed, he seemed thoroughly delighted. His own vast balloon-glass was barely moistened and as disregarded as Promethea's; he gazed at us somewhat, and somewhat more at his cheval-glass where he could see all three of us reflected, himself in famous company; he listened avidly, rapt, and missed the point entirely. Each separate point he missed, as I drove it home.

Prick, prick. I slid my needles in with the punctilious care of a practitioner, with the cold ruthless hand of an executioner. It was a revelation to me, that I could be so cruel; but this is why I take the drugs, to learn about myself as much as others, to see myself as they do, to set myself in their context far more than the reverse. It is in the nature of my work, after all, that I am always in their context.

At last, as the light-bar grew bright again beyond his polarising windows, Firensay shooed us gently to our beds. I was happy enough to leave the field by then, to leave my work, to leave Promethea gazing bleakly, drily after me. Where she would sleep, I didn't know; the day-bed in that hall might be her night-bed also, the only one up to her heroic stature. For me there was a human-normal guestroom, heroic only in its acreage, the sheer distance I had to walk across thick carpet before I could drop my clothes on the floor and my body onto the bed, discard it for the night—or for the day, rather, for what hours of sleep I could seize against the bright day and the turning circle, against the thought of waiting Mel.

When I woke, I found that someone had been in while I was sleeping. In and out and in again, to take my clothes and launder them and bring them back, clean and pressed and folded.

I wished that I might leave no more mark on my host than he would leave on me, on what I wore. Small chance of that. When I rose, when I was washed and dressed—and what, did he keep a camera on his guests in their rooms too, to know this so exactly?—a servant with crow-feather eyes led me to breakfast in a salon, in his company again.

At least there was no sign of Promethea, we were both spared her vast and wounded presence. He wanted to talk, or rather he wanted me to talk, about other worlds and other arts: to give him hints—although he did not say so—where next to scatter his money, what next to acquire.

In fairness, I could do no less, though I hated to think of my friends' work being swallowed by the emptiness of this crowded house. I betrayed them to it, to him anyway, because they would appreciate the money and never see the harm. Then I started to make noises about leaving and at last, at long last he let me go.

Back to the alley, back to Ro's: and I couldn't swallow my impatience long enough to go inside, up to my own room. There was nothing for me there. Instead I thanked Bulgar and dismissed him, watched him roll his carriage out of sight and then deliberately walked past the hostel and in at the yard gate, the way Mel had taken last night.

Here was a stable yard in truth, with stalls and cobbles—not stone, no, as the stalls were not wood, as the building beside was not brick, all plass imitations—and a very genuine dung-heap in the corner.

And there was the boy Dolph, shovelling muck with his back turned to me; and there was Mel's cab, gleaming from his promised attentions; and there through an open stable door—with, yes, the two proper halves of it separately hinged—was Mel. Her hindquarters, at least, just visible in the last of the light.

Already, I knew her by her tail-end. It was what I'd seen most of, after all, during yesterday's long pull along the Row. Also it was the part in which I had least interest, about which I had most curiosity. I would need to resolve my ambivalence, or at least set it to one side: soon, sooner or later, sooner would be best . . .

I stepped into the shadows of the stall and spoke her name.

Her face came clear as she turned smiling into the light, glad no doubt to have her fare restored to her, his fee assured. She held one arm high over her head as she washed her armpit, as she went on washing it, quite unconcerned that I should catch her so. The breast-band was off, and she seemed no more troubled by that. "There's a light," she said, "if you want it. Switch just on the wall there, by your elbow."

I was no more body-shy than she was, it's not an attitude you can carry from one discard to another, again and again. It makes no sense. Less even for her than it ever did for me: this body of hers had known hands she'd never seen, touches she'd never felt. How could she be precious about it now?

I did pull both halves of the door closed behind me, conscious as I was of the boy in the yard, before I touched the switch.

She'd called this a stable. So had I, in my head, and so it was. But I'd seen stables for livestock on two dozen planets, more: stables for horses, for other cattle, for creatures I couldn't name or fully understand. This was—well, nothing like those.

Nor should it be, of course. Mel was a friend here, but her stall was fitted out for a customer, a paying guest. And yet also cattle, as she was; and her horse-half would need horse-comforts, which did mean a great bed of straw-substitute, what looked like extruded packing material. Low in absorbency, perhaps, but no matter. There was a gutter and drain by the door, where I guessed she would stale and drop her dung. And then kick the door, perhaps, to attract Dolph's swift attention; a girl who washed herself before the evening wouldn't want to sleep in the smell of it.

Perhaps she'd call him, more normally. There was a comm unit on the wall. That was what made this such a strange stable, inevitably, that it must cater to human needs too. There were cushions and quilts for her comfort, there was a screen for her entertainment, there was a kettle, a basin with taps, a mirror. Shelves and closet space. I wasn't sure how much use she had for closet space, there wasn't too much of her that called for clothing, but not every guest here would be a working girl. Or a centaur.

She interrogated me about my night on the high side, while she went on splashing vigorously, unashamedly, no more an exhibitionist than I was a voyeur. And, yes, no less also. Looking was my profession and the basis of my craft; being seen, being looked at was a good deal of hers. Cabbies here must trade on their appearance, on their exoticism, as much as everyone else did.

I watched her washing, and wondered how she groomed; and asked, in the end, because however limber she was, however long of arm and short of pony-body, she couldn't conceivably reach it all.

"Oh, we tend to stable together and groom each other. Away from home, there's usually a stable-lad who'll do it for a tip. Some who don't need tipping, though they're likely to end up with a bruised foot for taking liberties." She grinned, unworried, and stamped for emphasis. "Not that I care, but they need to learn. Dolph, now, he's a pet. Busy tonight, or he'd have offered. He'd come anyway if I called, but I don't like to take him away from his real work, what Ro keeps him for. I'll do what I can with long-handled brushes, but I guess I'll be a bit scruffy for you, out on the Row tonight. That's if you still want to go . . . ?"

"Oh," I said, "I definitely want to go. And I don't care, but you won't be comfortable out on show if you think you're looking scruffy. I'll help, if you tell me what needs doing."

"Oh no, you're my passenger . . ."

"You're my guide; I want you easy with yourself." And my practice was full-immersion, I needed individual intimacies as much as broad experience. I needed to feel how these bodies worked. Flesh and bone beneath my fingers, that disjunct where bare skin turned to hide and fur . . .

There were brushes handy on a shelf there. I took one and began to groom her flank, following the way the coat lay, brushing out a fall of dust and hair. "Is this right?"

"Unh, right brush, yes. Harder, though. If you're sure you don't mind."

"I don't mind. Just you mind to leave my feet intact; I don't know what's a pleasure for you and what's a liberty for me, you'll have to tell me. Nicely . . ."

Closeness and work and the weighty warmth of her; I hadn't accounted for weight, so scrawny she seemed in both girl and pony parts. She did have it, though, leaning into me, an animal response to the brush. Just as she had animal odours—in no way offensive, only emphatic—that contrasted oddly with her purely human teasing, the way she flicked her tail at me and suggested that when I was finished with that, I might like to polish her hooves . . .

I did comb out the tail, tugging mightily at tangles. Wherever my hands went they took no liberties, apparently; at least they invoked no crushing stamps in retribution. To me, it all seemed extraordinarily intimate, to her so everyday that she took advantage of my labours at her hind quarters, to get her eating done at the other end.

At first I thought she had a bucketful—and yes, it was a bucket, and yes, it was full—of pasta; but I went to look more closely, and actually it was beansprouts of some kind. She gestured, I sampled, and found them uninspiring.

She chewed, by the handful. And grinned at me, deliberately, with sprouts between her teeth.

"This much," I said, "every day?"

"Twice or three times a day, this much at least; and even that—well, you can see," a gesture at her leanness, "I should eat more. I should. I do try. Sometimes my jaw aches, just from the chewing. It's why Carmel passed this body on so quickly, poor little bitch, she couldn't bear this."

Rich little bitch, of course she could afford it. Not Mel. "Aren't there, I don't know, supplements? Boosters?" Of all the peoples on all the planets, stations, orbitals in the network, all the worlds the

Upshot found or founded, these here should be the ones who'd know best how to maintain a hybrid body. They should do better than this.

She fingered the sprouts, played with them; said, "These little beauties are the best we have down here, for herbivorous morphs. It's easier for carnivores, I think. Easier for everyone on the high side. Us, we get this. Packed full of good nutrition, everything a horse could want; just, a horse's digestion needs the bulk. You can't get around that. You have to chew. Hours, every day. While someone nice grooms your other flank, say, and your horse-belly . . . ?"

I chuckled, and nodded, and made my way around her hindquarters to do that. And *en passant* did that rump-slapping thing I'd seen so often from stockmen and cattleherds and grooms.

I hadn't seen any of their cattle lash back quite so fast, with a hoof shod in pastel plass. She aimed to miss, I think.

I want to think.

Laughing as I brushed her, feeling her own laughter beneath my hands, I asked, "Why do you do this, Mel? What's the appeal of a second-use body, with hooves? Why do you want to be a pack-animal tugging tourists about for small change, sleeping in stables, needing someone else's help to keep yourself clean?"

There must be an answer, whether or not she could articulate it. It was what I'd come in search of, what the art would examine. Even I wasn't usually so blunt, but this wasn't only for the art any more. For me, I wanted it from her: her motives, her own understanding, the reasons that took her into the Upchute with her next body chosen and waiting on the opposite arc of the Row.

She said, "Stallion sex, of course. You can't imagine, you wouldn't *believe* . . . It's bloody rough, mind, but fuck, it's good. I'm not sure I could ever go back to human-normal now, I'd miss it for *ever*."

And no, I didn't believe her, not for a moment. She was young, she barely knew me, why wouldn't she be facetious? She was skittish suddenly in the stall there, adolescent, aggravating: trying to sell it to me, exhibitionism and exotic sex as the two motive forces that kept this station spinning, but I wouldn't buy. Not that. Not that alone. I wanted more, and was determined to find it.

It's not ordinarily so hard to stay objective. My nature is to shy away from anything didactic, to bring no conscious agenda to the work. All art is an act of autobiography, of course, but it ought to be detached. My own discipline demands that; immer is mediated necessarily by insight, but should never be tainted with personality.

That night, I wasn't thinking clearly. I watched Mel make herself ready for the street—her human self, once her coat was brushed, her tail combed, her horse's belly filled—and wanted her to be bigger than she claimed. Older, wiser, deeper.

By her own account, by her own actions her life was all display still, surface tension. She brushed colour into her hair, then combed it into a gaudy crest; she offered me her spraysticks to paint her, face and body—"you're an artist, cut loose, enjoy yourself"—and when I declined she made a job of it herself, patterns that reached from her hairline above to her hairline below, just that little lower than her navel.

Satisfied at last, she flung on a gilet of purple leather—not for modesty, I thought, so much as the convenience of pockets; it barely covered her breasts when it hung straight, and swung open whenever she gestured, as she did often and broadly—and we were away.

She called it going out on the Row, but actually not if that central circuit, that roadway was the Row. Or the constant parade, if that was it, then still not. Where we went that night, we crossed the road time and again, but spent our time in the alleys and barns behind.

I've done that same thing—tasting the night life, the wild side, cheap and dirty, all edge and sting—on more worlds than I can count, in as many kinds of company, in pursuit of what I did or what I wanted, what I was.

None of it was anything, *anything* like being out on Rotten Row with Mel.

Again, it was the hybrid nature of the night that kept on startling me. I was hungry, and life in the alleys after dark was all about street food, wandering from stall to stall and sampling this, that, none of that—

"Oh yes," she said, "I've got a human stomach too, I can eat human food. I insist on it. I'm always hungry, y'know? Even once the horse-belly is full. Full as it gets, full as I can bear to fill it. Just, not meat," and she shuddered, and there was nothing theatrical in that, she meant it entirely—

—and I've done it all before, yes, with humans or with aliens or with both of those together; never with both combined into the one body. Going side by side with Mel was utterly different to sitting in her cab and being towed. She clopped like a horse, she talked like a girl; she looked like a girl, so long as I was looking up—she topped me by a distance, even with a short girl's torso erupting from a short pony's shoulders—but any other perspective brought me up against the animal, up short. And if I lagged, if I got distracted, then suddenly I was walking behind a horse, and had to skip on quickly because I didn't at all know how to deal with it.

When she said, "Climb on, you can ride me; I won't let you fall," I assumed she was joking. I hoped she was joking. I shook my head; she shrugged and clip-clopped ahead a little, just to make me skip again.

Certainly she wasn't joking when she said she was always hungry. However full she was with beansprouts, she still had a human palate coupled with a horse's appetite to graze. And she had a very human appetite for gossip, and she knew, oh, everybody. So it seemed.

"Mel! Mel, you'll take a bowl of kefu, won't you? Best on the Row, but you know that! Two bowls, will it be, one for your own self and one for your friend?"

I'm not a fool, I know when 'friend' means 'client, stranger, gull'; but Mel took a bowl and paid for it her own self, didn't look to me to buy her dinner. I had promised, but that was yesterday. Tonight I took her independence to be a sign of bona fides, and followed suit.

Kefu? I'd have called it soyblock studded with seaweed: rough cubes of textured protein, embedded with something green and salty—not a leaf, it had its own contrasting texture: crunchy between the teeth, slippery to the tongue—and served in a sauce that was dark and bittersweet.

The bowls were small. This was not meant for a meal; it was a taste, a flavour, something to carry forward. As we did, leaving that stallholder with the empty bowls and a smile from me, a kiss from Mel, buying a drink each from his neighbour—"this is shaltour, it's a fruit. Of sorts. What you do, you shake it up. Hard, like this. And then you punch one of these plass tubes through the shell, just here where the stalk was, where it's weakest"—and crossing the road again, looking for another flavour even as we sucked that down. Shaltour is spicy and dense, and ought not to be as refreshing as it is. It reacts, I think, chemically with human saliva, a forgery of cleansing ease.

And left us wanting something new, more, other; and here was a man selling thokto, which I'd have taken for dried eels at first glance and something more or less the same at first taste except that Mel demanded them, one for now and more for later, so they must be vegetation of some description. They were a long chew, fibrous and dry but dissolving slowly into gelatinous strings in the warm wet of a human mouth, and they inhabited a spectrum of flavours that was the sea entire, remote and iodine and mysterious.

"Where does all this come from, Mel?"

"Oh, all over." She shrugged with the insouciance of someone very young, who has given no thought at all to tomorrow, nor much to the workings of today.

"It's amazingly cheap for imports," and it was amazingly difficult to understand how imports could be commonplace, here on Rotten Row. Of course there would be trader captains who would come, far and slow, for money enough—for Promethea, sure, for Domo Firensay and his kind—but not for Mel and her kind, and not with thokto.

She tutted. "All over the Row, I meant. I'll show you, tomorrow. Tonight—well, look, there's Tojun . . ."

Tojun might have been an entertainment, might have been a food-stuff. As it turned out he was a person and a fire-juggler, which made him an amusement for the young, which meant Mel emphatically, but I thought not me. There were people who ate fire, who blew fire, who threw fire from hand to empty hand on the planet of my birth; there have been more on every planet, every settlement, every station I've passed though since.

I was ready to be bored, preparing myself for it, but like every-thing—everyone—here on Rotten Row, Tojun was different. He did it differently. Child of the phoenix, he grew fire like a blossom from his tongue; he spat it into his bare hands, and moulded it into flying figures and threw them high, and they circled overhead like paper aeroplanes on fire, and like paper aeroplanes on fire they were consumed and fell to ground, except that there was no ash.

It wasn't magic, of course, but it might as well have been. It wasn't for the natives, either, but again it might as well have been, at least for Mel. She loved the show, clearly and honestly; she applauded first and loudest, and then snatched the hat from his head and carried it around the gathered circle of tourists while he flung sheets of fire into the sky for encore.

And she was still doing that—bullying, cajoling, gleaning cash: revealing herself to be as much an artist as he was, manipulating

67

people as he did flame, and I wondered just how much she'd manipulated me already, how much more there was to come—when a bolt came down from heaven.

A hurtling thing, a shadow, dark as cursing. I saw it just at the last moment, striking out of the black sky into the light, into the fire.

Literally, into the fire.

And through the fire, of course, because that was only a sheet of flame, nothing solid; and so tumbling to ground with all its feathers aflame.

It fell into that open circle that Tojun's art had cleared, bird-man grotesquely burning, no conceivable part of the show.

People screamed and backed away: tourists mostly, in their human-normal bodies and their horrified state of mind. This was too close, too immediate. Physically dangerous, even, the way the creature was rolling across the circle, as though it wanted to share its flames, its dreadful fate around.

People screamed and stayed: morphs mostly, more used to visual shock and apparent pain but only used to watching it, applauding. This was the real thing and they had no experience, no resources.

People moved to help, a few: notably Tojun and Mel, and me. He was a firemaster with demonstrably flameproof skin, accustomed and immune. I was an artist and a traveller, and both those roles had brought me close to other people's calamities, often enough to be ready. Besides, those of us who stand back, who use what we see, we have an obligation to scorch our fingers when that's needed.

Mel was half-horse, physically more than half, and her hooves skittered anxiously, they wanted to be running; and she was half-naked, more than half, what did she have to offer? But she was there at my side as I stripped off my new coat—long and heavy, unnecessary, indulgent—and threw it down across the flaming agony that was the birdman. She was already stooping, reaching to help me roll him in the fabric, when Tojun flung himself between us, using all his body to smother the flames.

"Tojun, careful!" Mel cried out, anxious for everyone; holding my hand, I realised suddenly, unless it was me that was holding hers. "You know how frail his bones must be . . ."

Better crushed than roasted. Tojun didn't need to say it, to either of us. All he did was grunt before levering himself up onto hands and knees above the prone birdman, before beginning to peel my scorched coat away from him, to let the poor bird breathe; to reassure us all, perhaps, that he was still breathing.

Which he was, in a thin gasping way, ultimately distressed. His eyes were unreadable, dark and dull in the ruin of his face. The double ruin, I'd have said, first remade into this debauched, debased semblance of another creature's birthright, and now scorched featherless and worse, burned deeply, so that even as we watched it was blistering beneath pin-stubble and naked black-ened skin.

The chest was worse, where it had been naked to begin with and the fire had chewed straight through into flesh that was raw and weeping now. It seemed too much for that brief flash through a sheet of flame, he should not have burned this badly. Except that I thought I could smell something sharp and unnatural on him, an accelerant.

Either there was more than one of him, or else this was the same birdman, the eagle who had eaten Promethea's liver yesterday. Not that, perhaps, but something had poisoned him against his own life.

Mel said, "Lift him up onto my back, I'll take him to the Splice."

Stupidly, I said, "He needs a doctor."

She was more patient with me than I deserved. "Splicers are the best doctors we have. They make us these bodies, who else is going to know how they work or what they need? And *the* Splice, our Splice, she's the best we have, down low. She looks after us all."

Tojun was on his feet now, with the birdman all bundled up in his arms, in my coat. "She's right—but I'll take him."

"I'm quicker," Mel said, as though that were absolute.

"Yes, but you'd need me just to hold him on your back, so you'd have to go at my speed anyway. You couldn't carry both of us."

"I wouldn't let him fall."

"Then you'd be going really slowly, and it might as well be me that takes him. It's not far. If I'd just gone, I'd have been there before we finish arguing. You go home, Mel. Or have a drink, and then go home. See that she does that, would you?" he went on, turning to me. "Not more than one drink, mind. She's got no head for it, and steering a drunken horse back to her stable is no job you want, trust me . . ."

I was happy to trust him; happier that he was bearing the birdman away even as he said it; happier still that Mel protested no more than a stamp and a rude word yelled after him, that she didn't even start to follow. She was abruptly shaken and fretful, great horse-shivers running over her flanks and sending goosepimples up her arms, that she rubbed at ineffectually before she huddled them against her chest, hunched her spine, did all those things that would have made me put my own arm around her except—well, except that she was a centaur and all my notions of proportion were upset. I looked at her and what I saw was small, the girl of her; but the horse of her meant that she still stood a head taller than me and her shoulders where my arm belonged were out of my easy reach, out of my comfort zone.

Instead—it felt too intimate a gesture, uninvited, but I'd already been more intimate with her body, in the stables with the brush and comb—I reached out and put my hand on her back. Just where it curved abruptly, bone-crackingly upwards, rising between the horse's shoulders to become the girl. Just above the hairline, where warm chestnut coat gave way to the warm dark honey of her skin, just below the hanging hem of her gilet.

She didn't stamp, even in warning; she didn't pull away. For a moment she simply endured my touch, and I felt inadequate, almost meaningless, offering an impertinence in the guise of a comfort.

Then she turned towards me, leaned into me, her own arm came around my shoulders. It was a shocking inversion, all those disproportions underscored, but oh, it was welcome none the less. I was weirdly thrilled, adolescently excited that she should take my body for her solace; I embarrassed myself with my response, adolescent again. If I stood straight, my head reached that hollow between her shoulder and her neck and fitted neatly there. I stood very straight. I pressed close, my hand slid up her back and beneath her gilet, my other arm circled her waist; it was many times, in many ways inappropriate, but she seemed grateful for whatever contact we could manage. The more the better: she rubbed her cheek against my hair, and sniffled.

And said, "I'm sorry, I hated that . . ."

"Of course. Don't be sorry—except for him, I mean, that poor bird. It was hateful, what happened to him." And mysterious to the point of being incomprehensible, but that was for later.

"You're my client, I shouldn't . . ."

"Yes, you should." I held her more firmly to assert it, even though she showed no signs of pulling away. "We're doing this together, all of it. How else am I going to learn this place?"

I was learning strange, unexpected things from my own reactions: apparently I had a kink that had never had the chance to manifest before. I was attracted to the half-human, the exotic. The corrupt, by every definition that I knew.

No news, that there were those among the Upshot who were drawn this way. Half the tourists on Rotten Row were looking for some kind of sexual contact, and half the morphs on the streets tonight would be glad to provide it, for a consideration. I'd just never guessed that I'd be down among them.

Here I was, though, offering Mel thin reassurances and a tawdry physical comfort, and aching to offer her something entirely other. And feeling ashamed of myself, and adolescent again with no excuse for it; and absolutely not going to act on that particular impulse.

71

Young and robust this body might be, but sometimes even youth is no excuse.

Which didn't prevent my buying her a drink, the first alcostall we came to. We'd bypassed them earlier, because she wasn't interested and while I'm ever willing to try alien foods, alien ways of getting drunk are harder work and generally foul. This time, though, I stopped her by main force—well, a determined tug that she wasn't inclined to resist—and asked for something utterly evil and not in the least medicinal.

Which cost me little enough—here as elsewhere, incoherence apparently came cheap—and yielded up two small recyclable cups. They looked to hold dirty river water, brown and thin and not entirely pure. I thought there were things adrift in it, not quite floating to the surface. They might have been separate liquids, various in density or viscosity, not inclined to mix. I suppose.

It smelled—well, as predicted. Foul. But Mel took hers and knocked it back, still without letting go my shoulders; I felt the shudder well through her. And swallowed my nerves, and then my cupful; and—well, yes. As predicted.

When I could speak again, I said, "Another? Or shall we graze again?"

She smiled, and shook her head. "That's sweet, but Tojun did mean it. You don't want to escort a drunken horse. Or even a drunken girl with a horse's arse. Let's go home now. Ro'll see me right."

So we did that, with no more word or thought. Buskers and barkers and pimps, we passed them all; and Mel had a friendly word from half of them and barely acknowledged any, but kept me so close that I could feel their eyes on us, on me, all the way down the Row.

Did I see her to her stable, in some outbreak of chivalrous atavism, or did she simply neglect to let me go at the hostel doorway? Did I neglect to let go of her?

72

No matter. Some distinctions make no difference. We were there in that hybrid chamber, her space. Her horse-body folded itself neatly onto the bedding provided, which put her girl-body suddenly a metre lower than it had been, too low for me now where she had been too high before. She grinned up at me—she knew, she must know just how much I was struggling with the simple scalings of the Row—and reached to touch the call button on the comm.

"Dolph? Be a pet, bring me a bucket of kvass. You know how I like it: good and thick, warm, with lots of sops. And," glancing at me wickedly, "a skin of kumis for my friend. Don't bother with a glass."

She was feeling better, I guess, if she was prepared to tease. That was the upside.

Her order was delivered a minute later, prompt service for a favoured guest. I'm not naive, I am widely travelled and well read, well versed; I knew, more or less, what she was doing to me. What she was laying me open to.

Even so I let her explain it to me, spell it out. I thought she needed that, one more step away from what had happened on the street.

The boy brought a literal bucket that steamed gently in the stable's warmth. He also brought what looked like a bag of literal skin, of horse's skin perhaps.

She read my face, I think, and laughed at me. "Oh, what, are you thinking I'm a cannibal? Not me, sweet. That's for you. And no, it's not been cut off a horse. Or a centaur. They grow the skin in labs, because kumis doesn't taste right unless it matures in a mareskin. They grow the kumis too, sort of. I don't know. That's science, and I just pull a rick; but the milk comes out of the same lab as the skin, and no mares have been milked to get it. They could ask us, I suppose," and she paused, to peer back to where her hind leg covered her udder, her teats, "but they'd have to pay us, and I bet this is cheaper. Try, anyway. Fermented mares' milk."

I knew that. It's always worse, when you know in advance what they're giving you.

I hefted the skin, which bobbled and flexed fatly in my hands. "Uh, how . . . ?"

"See the nipple?"

I did: a bone or fake-bone plug, it was stitched and sealed into one corner.

"Pull it out—with your teeth is the classy way—then hoist the skin up high and catch the jet in your mouth. It's a good idea to spit the plug into your hand first, before you do the hoisting."

She was utterly enjoying herself, waiting to see me spill. Which I would, undoubtedly. I said, "You're not joining me?"

"No. Too close to cannibalism. Or autophagy, or something. I couldn't. I'll stick to kvass—fermented bread, basically. Not much alcohol, lots of substance. The way I take it, at least, there's lots of substance. For other people they filter out the bread, but I need all the carbs I can get. For me, they put in extra."

I could see dark and heavy sops floating like croutons on a thick soup. It looked more like porridge than beer; for her horsey self, I'd have been tempted to call it a mash. She was going at it already, with a spoon the size of a ladle. She'd slipped her gilet off first, not to splash on it; I thought perhaps I ought to do the same, but I didn't want to spoil her joke.

Out with the plug, then, in approved toothy manner. Up with the bag, and tilt: and yes, I did spill. It came at me in a spurt, fine and fast and almost impossibly hard to steer, to control from the heavy flex of the bag. It hit my chest first, my new shirt, where I was coatless; then it went over my shoulder in a stream; then it struck my face, and stung as it spattered.

Mel, of course, was in hysterics, choking over her own brew. Which was, of course—of course!—what I'd been playing for. I soaked myself with satisfaction, and promised myself and my shirt a long soak in water later.

When I did finally catch some of the kumis in my mouth, it was sharp and sour, thinner and less obviously milky than I'd expected.

No less foul for that, but I could bear it: for her entertainment, for my own pride, for something.

For her company, perhaps, for the right to be with her, here, where if anywhere she had a right to be private from her passengers.

She flicked her tail at me and said, "Sit. No, not there," as I made a move towards the chair that helped to make this a most unusual stable stall. "Sit with me."

Sit in her bedding, she meant, with my back against her shoulder, her horse-shoulder where it was warm and firm and animal. And yet also her, very much a part of her: and hence also embedded with her superficial enchantment and her far deeper need, and with the allure that reached to me regardless, which she knew nothing about, which I ought to be horrified to discover in myself but yet couldn't be, not here, now . . .

I said, "I'll cover you with kumis."

"I'll live with it. Dolph can sponge it off me in the morning. Sit."

Force majeure applied, though the forceful part of her was almost petite. I sat. And felt the twitch in her hide as I settled against her, and struggled not to misunderstand it, not to read it as an echo of my own swallowed eagerness. She was young, and hopefully not sensitive, still unrefined; I gave myself away no doubt in every minute, every movement, and could only trust that she wasn't subtle enough to read me yet.

She was above me again, rising up narrow-waisted from the barrel body of her pony self, and it all seemed very strange and very potent. What couldn't be potent was the kumis, there's not enough sugar in milk to make it alcoholically significant; and yet I felt drunk, I was acting drunk, tipping my head back and back, beaming up at her. Tipping the bag too and trying to snare that stream of kumis in the trap of my mouth, and then not quite managing to stop before I had to swallow, and so spraying both of us again.

And again.

She said, "You'd better take that off," turning in that alarming rubber-spined way she had, plucking at my shirt, "before you ruin it altogether. Put it to soak in a bucket, and have another drink."

One shoulder was sodden already, and the rest was splashed. I was singularly aware, though, that she was herself naked, at least to the waist, to the hairline. I was long past getting obsessed by a pert female breast—or I thought I was, I had been sure of it—but I was also achingly, preternaturally aware that breasts were all she had of normal human sex-stuff. Well, breasts and skin and hair. And a mouth, and hands, and . . .

"And what," I said thickly, "will Dolph sponge me too in the morning?"

"I'm sure he would, if you paid him. If that's what gets you off."

She knew that was not what got me off. Also, no way was I taking off my shirt—except that she was doing it herself suddenly, and I did seem to be cooperating.

And there was kumis in my hair, apparently, and she was rubbing at it with the dry tail of the shirt before she tossed it aside, no thought of actually setting it to soak in a bucket; and she said, "Stay," almost at the same time as I said, "Mel, I'm not—well, I'm not a stallion, y'know?"

She laughed softly, almost painfully, and said, "I do know that. It's all right. There is still fun to be had, even at this end."

I was sure of it, if she was; but, "I'm your client, Mel . . ."

"And what, you're worrying about your ethics? Or mine? When I'm in harness, between the shafts of my rick, I'm a cabbie and you're my client. When I'm being a guide, you're still my client. When you're in my stall here, you're my friend. I hope you're my friend. I don't invite clients in here, to do this." And then, "Oh. You weren't wondering how much you had to pay me, were you? Because—"

"Mel," I said quickly, almost truthfully, "I was wondering whether I had to ask for my money back. To avoid confusion."

"Oh," she said. "Nah, you don't have to do that. What we negotiated, that's the fee for what we negotiated. You can even tip me, if you like. This—"

"Ow!"

"—this is something else. Not something extra. This is for you, for me, for tonight," *because I need it* was what she didn't say, but I heard that anyway. She wanted company, distraction; not much more, I thought. No matter.

What I wanted—well, that was moot. There was advantage, work, art to be had from here, no doubt, but that wasn't why I stayed. There was physical pleasure too, and curiosity to be satisfied, and the same applied.

I thought I stayed for her, or I wanted to think so. I made it so, as best I could. Not being a stallion.

Afterwards—her not being quite a girl—we weren't quite able to spoon or snuggle into sleeping, but I was happy enough nesting deep in the bedding and warm against her ribs, against the hot heavy flesh and the slow rhythms of her breath and blood.

Morning brought—as mornings should, in stable yards—the sounds of industry, bucket and shovel and hose. These were followed, more unusually, by a quiet knock on the stall door. "Can I come in?"

"Yes, of course," Mel called, where I would have said the opposite.

Dolph opened the top door and wished us both good morning, asked if we were ready for breakfast, as polite and casual as if this were a double room in the hostel. Which effectively it was, I supposed, or we had made it so. It occurred to me that this was not the first time he'd caught Mel in company; indeed, that it was nothing out of the way.

Necessarily, then, it occurred to me that perhaps this was sometimes a part of Mel's contract with her clients, those tourists who came here for the kink of it. She rented out her body's strength, to pull people around in the rickshaw; why wouldn't she rent out her body's intimacies afterwards, or some small aspect of them? Dolph would be more intimate with her, every time he groomed her hindquarters.

I was sure of it suddenly, and as untroubled as I was certain. She hadn't adopted a fake offence when the subject of payment had risen obliquely between us last night; she'd just made it sweetly clear that it was an irrelevance, it didn't apply. Not to me. She'd wanted a friend, needed one, found one. I was happy with that.

Mel had her staple beansprouts for breakfast. I had bread and honey and fruits on a tray; no meat, I'd stressed that, while Mel laughed at me, mocking my careful sensitivity. She mocked me for my hunger too, but she was just as quick to start eating and even more reluctant to stop, finishing my tray after her bucket.

When finally we were both done, we went out into the yard where Dolph was waiting bare-chested with his hose at the ready and a long-handled brush.

I'd have enjoyed getting hot and wet with Mel, at least as much as the boy would, but the mixture of hope and baffled expectation in him was irresistible. I grinned at her sideways, and left her to his energetic mercies; went up to my own room to get hot and wet on my own account, on my own, under my own hard shower.

And so dressed, and carried my own bags down all those stairs to street level. And found Ro, and paid my bill and made a valiant effort to pay Mel's too, only that he would not take the money. Instead he waved me impatiently out of there, out into the yard, where I found Mel groomed till she gleamed, but not harnessed between the shafts of her equally gleaming rig. Instead she was waiting by the gateway, swatting cheerfully at Dolph as he fussed around her, as he gave one last brush to her coat, as he threatened to do the same thing to her hair.

In lieu of being allowed to pay her reckoning, I tipped the boy lavishly. Too lavishly, to judge by his expression and hers. He was awestruck; she rolled her eyes, tutted loudly, made a pantomime of it. Then she cuffed poor Dolph and warned him not to raise his expectations, not every guest would be such a moron with money. Then she ruffled his hair, which he clearly hated, which was clearly why she did it; then she kissed him, which made him blush ferociously, and he hated that too; then, at last, she glanced around and gestured to me, a beckoning twitch of her head.

"Aren't we taking the cab?"

"Not right now. I'm going down to see the Splice, ask how that idiot from last night is doing. I thought you'd like to come along."

Oh. Yes, of course she'd do that. Even at the cost of her hiring-fee, if she'd misread me entirely; her air of mild defiance made that clear.

I gave her nothing to defy. "Thanks, yes. If you don't mind. It's, um, personal for you, I think . . ."

"It's personal for both of us. You were there too; that was your coat he ruined."

Neither of us cared a damn about the coat, but it was something to hold on to. "Right, yes. Of course it was. What shall I do with my bags?"

"Sling 'em in the cab there. They'll be safe enough. Dolph'll keep an eye open, won't you, sweetheart?" Her young slave would do anything, clearly; he nodded with mute and helpless vigour. To me she said, "I don't know if we will move on tonight, actually. Well, you could go on by yourself, of course, there are other cabs, but . . ."

"No," I said. "I can wait till you're ready. But that," I stumbled between 'bird' and 'man', and settled for neither, "that morph won't be well for a long time, weeks," if he'd even survived the night, which I was inclined to doubt.

"We'll see. Come on, then, if you're coming."

Walk with me she meant, her hand said, a reaching invitation. I took it, and let her tug me out into the alley.

"If we stay another night," she said, as soon as we were out of earshot, "at least you'll be sure of right royal treatment."

I thought I'd had that anyway, simply by virtue of being with her; but I said, "How much did I give him?"

"A year's salary, more or less. It's dreadful pay, of course. Ro feeds him and houses him and expects him to live on tips, which is why we all tip him—but not like that. He's a good boy, though, he'll put it away. He's saving for his first morph, did you know?"

Of course he was. Why wouldn't he be? All the smart kids were. She was saving, I knew, for her next.

I was helping. More, I was validating her choices. Not that she needed validation from me, or from anyone. Even so I felt soured this morning, as much as I felt sated.

And still I clung to her hand and let her lead me: out onto the Row—of course! how else should we go anywhere, except in plain sight?—and some little distance before she drew me off down another side alley.

This one had no convenient signs to help you find the Splice; you knew how, or you didn't. Indeed, it was almost blatantly a secret. Halfway down the alley was the blank gable wall of a godown, with an unforthcoming steel door pulled shut. Mel let go of me, because she needed both hands to slide that aside. Beyond was an unexpected light and an almost startling ramp, curling down into that same light.

The ramp was ridged and textured, good for hooves, for claws, for any kind of feet. The way was broad enough for two to walk abreast, or for one very broad morph to go alone. Mel closed the door behind us and claimed my hand again, and down we went.

Down and around, down and around. I said, "How deep does this go?"

"Nearly there. But we've got Underside works all around the Row, it's like a second level that the tourists never see. That's how this place functions. Everything we eat is grown below the road, so's everything we wear, almost everything we use."

When she said everything they wore, she meant their bodies, mostly. That was clear, simply from the way she said it.

The ramp debouched us into a foyer, where broad doors were again closed against us. This was a medical seal, though, jurisdictive perhaps but not interdictive. The doors slid open at our approach, almost the first automation I'd seen on the station; these people restricted their power and technology to where they were most needed, and otherwise relied on horsepower and servants.

We walked forward at the doors' implied invitation, and a cold antiseptic light washed over us. Standard superficial sterilisation, clothes and skin: elementary among the Upshot, but here I was enough attuned to the primitivisms of the Row that I startled at it.

Mel was expecting it, of course, and didn't flick an eyelid or kick a hoof. Conspicuously so, I thought.

Beyond that barrier, was it a hospital or a laboratory? Or a morgue? I couldn't decide. Well, I could decide against the last; there was nothing of death here. Except that there were bodies that had no life, and by Mel's own report some of those had lived before. Even if they were being kept in anticipation of future use, it still stank to me of death and worse, reanimation. I could understand the rationale and the drive to do that, in a place so economically and morally shiftless; in Mel—because I am no less a hypocrite than anyone else, and because the regime of immersive hypnotic drugs makes me vulnerable, and for a hundred reasons else—I could excuse it. I still thought it was a vile practice.

There were other bodies, others' bodies here in the familiar tanks, still growing or fully grown and waiting for decant. Most claimed already, no doubt, bespoke; some, I supposed, in the tank for the second time or more, awaiting takers. A glance wouldn't tell me which was which, and I had no desire to look. Some—most—of those tanks were oversized. To meet these people in the living flesh was shocking and wonderful; to see them in embryo or any stage beyond, immersed in vat-fluids like specimens preserved—no.

I couldn't bear it. Especially not to turn from that to this, from bottled freaks to Mel.

Besides, we weren't here on tour. For once, I was not thinking to make art. There were benches of instruments and screens to one side, the tools of the gene-splicer, behind a wall of clear plass and another sealed door; that really was the laboratory, where these rampant, monstrous morphs were sown, sewn, human and animal and artificial DNA grafted all together. I ought to have been fascinated by the process, no doubt I could and would be, only not today. Not with Mel at my side, someone coming to greet us and a figure lying prone on a medical table behind her, swathed in a gel-soaked sheet.

The figure's shape through the sheet was diagnostic, even before we were close enough to see the face. What there was, what there ever had been that could be called a face; what there was left of it now.

Just the shape of the skull was a giveaway.

I'd thought this an errand of futility, of mourning, a duty-call to mark the sad strange death of a stranger. I thought the fall, the plunge from on high should have killed him, as it was surely meant to, before the flames had their chance; I thought the flames should have killed him too, before the rough handling that came after; I thought that if both of those first two had failed, then the third should have finished him off. Bird-bones are notoriously frail, they have to be, to keep the body light enough to fly. The hugely heavier Tujon had crushed him in my coat and rolled on top of him after, heedless of what damage he himself was doing. Half the birdman's bones should have been broken already, from the fall; after that rough salvation, I'd envisaged punctured lungs and ruptured organs. One dead birdman and one body ruined past mending, not fit for passing on.

It was good to be wrong, of course it was; but I watched the morph's chest rise and fall beneath his winding-sheet, and it was astonishing and shocking and very particularly wrong itself.

The drugs I take for immer eat my mental skins away. One of those is what protects me otherwise from sinking into other people's pain; another is what keeps me socialised, able to deal with new-met people on those superficial levels, day to day.

Mel had to nudge me physically out of staring at the birdman, absorbing the fact of him, the every breath of his survival. She had to lean her horse-heavy shoulder against mine and say, "Hey, are you *listening* to me? This is the Splice, I thought you wanted to meet her?"

"Yes—yes, of course. I'm sorry." A short woman, barely more than shoulder-height to me, and this wasn't a tall discard they'd given me. Short and curious, to see me in Mel's company: waiting, I thought, to learn why I was there, as potential customer or critic or something other. There was something bizarre about her, that took me a moment to understand. And then I didn't understand myself, because in fact she was utterly human-normal, at least to my eyes, and that was the bizarrerie.

Had I immersed myself so far, so soon? Was I really so ready, so quick to see variation as the norm, to find an unexaggerated body unusual?

There were tourists, and then there were residents. There were the young, like Dolph, and then there were adults. And here was the second resident adult who wore a body unmodified, so far as I could tell by looking; and yes, this time, that had seemed really strange.

In honesty it still did, even once the moment had passed. Later would be the proper time to think about that, perhaps the proper time to ask. Now was neither.

I've been on stations where you greet a stranger by flashing your profile from your dataset to theirs, all the information you're ready or willing to make public, plus all that you're obliged to, willing or not. I've been on stations where that would be redundant, where you know that the controlling hi-hal has done that thing already because it's done the same thing in reverse and you already know so much about the person approaching—and they about you—that it's almost impossibly hard to think of them as a stranger at all.

Here, in good keeping with the archaisms that pervaded Rotten Row, introductions were apparently slow and personal, short on data and consonantly high on social status. Perhaps that was only a measure of how much Mel respected this woman, but it felt right to me, appropriate and genuine both.

Mel said, "Here she is, then. Splice, meet duLaine, who's an Upshot artist of some complicated kind that he will certainly explain to you with all the science added, if you give him half a chance. duLaine, this is Dr Huevinnen Corossa, also known as the Splice. Dr Corossa is a geneticist, whose work is published all through human space; the Splice runs the best morphing clinic on the Row."

"By which she means," Dr Corossa interrupted, "the best that she and her disreputable friends can afford."

"That's not what I mean at all. It's true, but that's not the point. If we were rich, if we were highsiders, we'd still be coming here."

"If you were highsiders, my sweet, you'd be fetching me up to you."

"We wouldn't need to; you'd be up there already yourself, not forced to work down here in the Underside. We'd see that you had all the room and resources that you deserve. Which you could do anyway, if you didn't choose to hang with us disreputable types."

This was an old conversation, all too clearly. Not even an argument, just a place they tended to visit. Dr Corossa shrugged it off, no time for wish-fulfilment. She turned to me and said, "Excuse me, we'll talk properly in a minute; but I don't believe that Mel came here today to introduce me to a new friend, however fascinating he might be."

"Or fascinated—but you're right, of course. Not our primary purpose. We both of us came to see how your patient is progressing—"

"—he was there, he helped," Mel asserted vigorously, "it was his coat that Tojun used to smother the flames—"

—which effectively pointed out how little help I'd been, because fireproof Tojun could have used anything including his own bare hands, which I guessed had had their building here; but I smiled my thanks at her and went on, "I'm impressed by the quality of your care. More than impressed," *astonished*, but it would have felt rude to say so, "because honestly, I never thought he'd survive what we saw him go through," fall and fire and the smothering after.

"Oh, they're tough," she said, "these children," and I thought she meant *my children*, I thought she wanted to claim them all. "Besides, this lad was made on the high side, the signs are all over him."

Not one of hers, then, except in her sympathies. "I'm sorry," I said, "I don't know what that means," what it was meant to signify. Clearly something more than a maker's mark.

"Over-engineered," she said bluntly. "It's the rarified atmosphere up there, I think, they grow too fond of artifice and complexity. Their work is clever, of course, but they don't know where to stop, when they have no need to. Given everything they need and more, everything they ask for, they spoil their morphs the same way they're spoiled themselves. Everything is made way beyond spec, just because they can afford it. Luxury models, for their luxury clients and their servants too. Even for an actor in a pageant, who needs nothing more than flight and appetite. This poor boy is put together with all the resilience of a bridge. He's got plass in his bones."

I misunderstood, of course, I thought that was a metaphor until Mel stamped a hind leg and said, "Well, so have I."

"Yes—and you don't really need it, you came out of the same stable. Over-engineered, as I said. In your case they had at least some excuse. Two excuses: that spine would be hard to structure or support in simple bone—which is the technical excuse—and they were at least making that body for a daughter of the house, which means they would naturally be catering to the most absurd demands, her every whim satisfied, regardless of necessity or good design. This lad's been heaving himself about with ridiculous reinforcement, simply because it was an interesting challenge and the client was sure to pay for it. As it happens, it saved his life—but only because he tried to take his life, so his survival doesn't look like much of a blessing, does it?"

That was a question I didn't want to face, any more than Mel did. Life was life; what else was there? There could always be another body, another kind of life. Especially for him, who had been living within such limits. Change was his only choice, or seemingly so. Instead he'd opted for the other thing, the change beyond choice, out of all choices . . .

I said, "How do you put plass in someone's bones?"

The doctor shrugged in that way specialists have, who want to say *it's too complicated for you to understand*. It was Mel who snorted and said, "Why not? It's a compound, it grows, it has a DNA. The Splice can graft that in, the same way she grafts everything."

Which was obviously painfully simplistic to Dr Corossa; it was a little glib even for me. But I didn't have that stuff in my bones, and I was glad to move even further from topics we none of us wanted to talk about. I said, "Don't you mind, that they call you Splice?"

"*The* Splice," Mel growled, with a sideways toss of her eyes, of her glare. "The only one that counts."

"The one that works for street prices, she means. And gives credit."

"That's not what I mean, and you know it . . ."

"No, all right. That's not what you mean." The doctor turned away from us both, towards her patient, *this is what you mean* spelled out in clean and minimal movements. "I'm glad you came to see him; he'd appreciate that, if he were conscious. I think he'd appreciate that." Though he couldn't say so, obviously. He had no means to express it: only a beak that would never form words, claws that could not hold a pen or work a keypad. Otherwhere, other societies might have— did have—more sophisticated means to read a mind or transmit a desire, an intent. Not here. Here they were ironically locked within their bodies, choosing and designing limits for themselves, having the doctor and her like generate the vessels of their own containment.

"Will he recover?"

"Oh, yes. I think so. From the burns, at least, and the other physical damage. That much I can address. His mental state is beyond my competence."

And he had tried to kill himself, that was beyond dispute; and if we couldn't address that, then the strength of his internal structures and the quality of the doctor's care all went for nothing, as did our own small efforts to save him on the night.

Mel said, "Do you have any idea . . ."

". . . why he did it, why he'd choose to die? Not a one. If he was conscious, he'd have no way to tell me. But we know whom he served, and what he did for her. I sent Tethys to learn what he can."

"What, wait," I said, "my Tethys? I mean, the Tethys I met in reception?"

"Yes," the doctor said, "I expect so. He does a lot of work around the 'chute. It pays well, and he needs the money."

"For his wings. Right." She was likely the mentor he'd spoken of; mentor and engineer both. "Does Tethys know—uh, this guy, I'm sorry, I don't know his name?"

"None of us does. Not even Tethys, no. Whoever he is, he'd had no bird-morphing before, or I'd have known about it. That might be another reason for the over-engineering, to build him a body he could be sure to fly in, first off. It's easier without arms in the equation, of course: remapping the neural pathways from arms to wings is straightforward. But Tethys is . . . sentimental, about birds. I think he envied this lad from the first, I think he'd have swapped in a moment. When he heard about last night, he was straight here. I've sent him off where he can be some use, maybe; that boy has a sharp ear for gossip, and all the contacts he'll need to pick it up."

I was sure of that, and just starting to wonder about something else. I looked at Mel and said, "You know Tethys too, do you?"

She had the grace to blush. When a centaur blushes, with all that weight of horseblood behind the impulse—well. Scarlet actually is the word for it. Regular blushing humans are positively pallid in comparison.

"Yes," she said, "of course I do. Anyone who spends any time with the Splice, we all hang out together . . ."

"Make a nuisance of yourselves," Dr Corossa said, allegedly to her, in fact just in support of her, trying to divert me, "get in my way, drive me halfway out of orbit comparing morphs and arguing whose is smarter, who's best articulated, what you should all aim for next . . ."

I said, "That's all very cute, but the doctor didn't even make your morph, Mel, you told me that yourself."

"No, it's highside work. Right. So what? The Splice keeps me working—"

"Basic maintenance," Dr Corossa said, "basically she means I keep her in pretty shoes, there's little else needs doing—"

"They are pretty, aren't they?" Mel danced on her hooves, cocked one back to admire the ridged plate fixed somehow to the sole, did her very best to distract me. Didn't work, except for that brief moment where I wondered why the shoes weren't built into her coding, if she could have plass built into her bones. But then, no doubt the Carmel who'd had that body before her would never have wanted practical shoeing, fit for real work on the Row.

Not distracted, no. I said, "So you and Tethys hang out together, here or anywhere—and you want me to believe it's sheer coincidence that five minutes after I leave Tethys in reception, it happens to be you that comes along with your cab, looking for a fare?"

"Oh, the Row's a small habitat, we all know each other . . ."

"None of you knows him," with a nod to the figure on the bed.

"No, but that's freaky, that's the odd thing, not me and Tethys. Besides, I'm a cabbie; where else am I going to hang around? I get all my best fares from reception."

"Oh, I'm sure. I just think you get all your best fares from Tethys, I think he tips you off."

She hesitated, glancing sideways, as if looking for Dr Corossa's approval or consent to the confession. That seemed strange to me, where none of the rest of this did at all. Then she shrugged and said, "Well, maybe. Does it matter?"

Originally, not at all. One petty little conspiracy: why not? It was doubtless one among a thousand, all the population of the Row teaming up to find advantage, working together to extract as much cash as possible from the tourists and keep it for preference among their friends.

Except that Mel had not only trotted me along the Row, she'd welcomed me to her stall last night; and if she took no money for it I still thought that was exceptional, circumstantial, not her usual practice. Now I thought, I had to think perhaps that was the tip that Tethys gave her, *here comes a tourist who'd be up for more than a ride*; and I was suddenly angry with him for thinking it and angry with her for pursuing it, angry more with myself for proving them both right.

And after a day and a night with Mel, all that physical and verbal intimacy, coupled with the more rarified empathic effects of my drugs, I knew this wasn't all. There was something yet that she was more ashamed of. That the doctor knew about, and didn't want me to discover; which meant surely that it was something to do with discards, no, decants they called them here, and—

And I was clenching my jaw already against an acid bile rising, but I did have to ask, I had to force the words out, even while I was desperately casting about to find the door to a toilet, to a bathroom, to anything semi-private and easily scrubbed.

I said, "You don't, after the tourists leave, you don't discard their bodies," don't crush and carbonise to a solid numbered recorded disc as the Upshot always have, as our law demands. "Do you?"

"No." I was looking at Mel, but it was Dr Corossa who answered, cool and matter-of-fact and understanding me, knowing what came next. "We can't afford the waste, on Rotten Row. We don't discard anything that we can use again."

"Tourists come and go," Mel said, catching on slowly. "A day sometimes, a few days, almost never longer than that. Of course we keep the decants."

"And use them again."

"Yes. Of course. For the tourists. Why not? One body can host, oh, I don't know, dozens, before it starts to degenerate. Splice?"

"More than dozens," Dr Corossa said, watching me.

And I was only talking now, I was ahead of myself as I was ahead of them, but I did have to say the words.

"This, then," and I almost didn't have the words after all, I almost tried to make do just with the gesture, a sweep of my arm to take in the body that I stood in, young and fit and human-normal, just as any tourist would demand, "this *decant* that you gave me, it's been used before, am I right?"

"Yes, of course," again from Dr Corossa, patient and deliberate and forthright. "Certainly, I should say so. We don't grow new decants for the tourists any more, we don't need to; we have enough. And work enough to do, thank you. Of course we recycle when we can, as often as we can."

Recycle. Even recycled flesh, it seems, even a much-used body will still react to our own revolted instincts, what we bring fresh to it.

Under compulsion, it turns out you can clench more than your jaw. Jaw and throat, from the gullet all the way down to the stomach, I clamped it all in a determined, desperate seize and dived for the nearest open doorway.

I was lucky, though I'd been looking for my luck. This was a shower-room, with a drain in the middle of the floor. There was a door to close behind me, but I couldn't spot the mechanism in the moments that I had before my body—mine? no, not mine even in the usual discard sense, one-use only: this was something other and I couldn't get my head around it, it couldn't contain me, not possibly—this vessel of flesh overrode my frantic control of it. I was working against myself, I knew, and the body was only the medium that lay between us, between me and me, but even so—

Even so, I spewed a thin stream of bitter, burning bile onto the floor and into the drain. Hunched over it, hands on knees and spewing, spitting, tears running from my eyes as my belly spasmed and my throat filled again.

Behind me, I was aware first of the silence, and then of voices murmuring; then footsteps quietly coming after me. Hoofsteps. I'd thought it would be Dr Corossa, but no. No compromise, making nothing easy: *let's not soften reality with a human-normal confidante,* they might have said to each other, *let him deal with what it is, full-face . . .*

Both of us, it seemed, we had to face each other. It wasn't easy for Mel, perhaps, any more than it was for me, standing there amid the stink and spatter of my vomit. She had that to face and also her own complicity, just as I had embarrassment and humiliation on top of the revulsion that I had to confront with every breath and every movement. Knowing that others had breathed with these same lungs, moved this same body to their own desires.

Realising suddenly one more thing that it meant, that it might mean; staring at Mel and wondering how to ask . . .

She had practical measures in hand, a glass of water and a towel.

"Don't say anything yet. Here, just swill and spit."

I did that gratefully. Then I reached for the towel, but she wouldn't let me take it. Instead she worked it roughly over my face and head, nothing hesitant or gentle, rubbing scratchily at sweat-slicked skin and hair.

"Better now?"

"Yeah. I guess . . ." I did feel better, at that moment, but I was still only guessing. Could I live like this, could I inhabit a body that disgusted me, or would I just have to spew again and again until I made it back to the 'chute and away from here? Could I even speak to these people who were at least complicit in what had been done to me . . . ?

I took a sip and decided that I could. I could swallow water, at least, and it needn't come up again instanter. Which being true, I could likely talk as well. And she was close, right there, and I wanted not to talk at all; I wanted to hit her, rage at her with my fists, except that every blow would be a reminder that this was not my body at all, that these hands had done other things with other people's purposes behind them. And I wanted to hold her, to hug her, to lean all my weight of sorrow and distress on her strong young resilient body with plass in its bones, I wanted to give myself over to her as I had last night, dependent and exhausted and in thrall.

And of course I did neither of those, I just spoke to her; I said, "Did you, have you known this body before? With, with someone else inside it?"

A half-smile twisted her mouth. "I wondered if that would be bothering you. Along with everything else that bothers you, I mean. No, I haven't. But I might have done, you do need to understand that."

Oh, I did, I understood it entirely, it was inherent. To my drugged-up senses, it made an entirety of sense. "It's happened before, I expect?"

"Yes," flatly, no equivocation.

"And you've, um, slept with them? The same body but different, different people?"

Her air was a little puzzled, a little amused, as though she wanted to ask if that really mattered so much; but that might have seemed like equivocation, so, "Yes," she said again, just as flatly.

The silence was heavy between us for a minute, and when I broke it, I did it violently, flinging a hard little word at her the way I might have liked to fling a stone, sharp-edged and looking to break something. "Why?"

Her shrug said she did it for the money, it said she did it for the fun, or for the comfort, or for the simple desire of it, for all the reasons that people do; it didn't understand why I was asking.

"No," I said, "not you. I mean, why do so many people want to sleep with you?"

"Oh, thanks," she said, and folded her arms and stamped a dainty hoof in a teasing outrage at my gaucherie.

"No, stop it. I'm serious."

"You're not the only one in the universe to find me attractive, you know. Not even the only one on Rotten Row. Assuming that you do find me attractive, of course. Beast."

And those who could be attracted to a morph, to a hybrid, would naturally gravitate here, and a lot of them would find her, or she them, simply by the nature of her work; and even so, she was hiding something. And she was available, clearly, unworried about using that exotic body any way that it could be used, for money or for pleasure or whatever came her way; and even so, she was hiding something. Turning away to touch a button that did cause a door to slide across the opening, lifting a hose with a shower-head from the wall, using a jet of water to rinse my vomitus off the floor and down the drain, threatening my feet playfully, hiding something.

"And what does it matter, anyway," she said determinedly, "if someone else had use of that body before you? It's like rooms, like clothes—or are you fussy about clothes too, do they have to be new too? There's nobody but you in there now, which is what's important, surely. You're the only one feeling what you're feeling. You're the one who's going to feel soaked," another twitch of the water-jet, "unless you start acting nicer."

She said that, but she dialled up a stronger jet and turned it deliberately on her own legs, her own hindquarters; and she stood there stamping and splashing in the spray, grinning at me through the backwash, the very image of a wise young soul thoroughly at ease inside a body that had been used before and was now her own, at least until she chose to pass it on.

She was wise inside, perhaps, but not so much. She had no idea what I was feeling: how much I wanted her to make good her threat, to turn that wand of water in my direction and soak me so thoroughly there'd be nothing to do but strip to my skin and see what happened when we were warm and wet and naked together. Right there in the doctor's surgery, in her shower-room, behind the token privacy of a door that could no doubt be opened from either side without benefit of locking. The way I was feeling, I didn't care. This decant, this body of common use could revolt me no more naked than it did already, it could be no more exposed. Given how many strangers had seen it already, seen it and worn it and used it, abused it—given that lost history, what could it matter if I abused it now, if I was gross and gauche and demanding, if the doctor knew? If the doctor watched, if she cared to? She might be interested, technically, to see how a human-normal and a morph found ways to couple. She might just be a voyeur. After all, she did her thing here, she made her morph bodies and chose not to use one herself. Looked like a voyeur to me, and I should know . . .

I used to say my drugs give me intimate distance, letting me share motives and emotions without being truly involved. How else could I make art, I used to say, without that dual tug of observation and engagement, without the dichotomy?

Here, I couldn't find a balance either way. This decant disgusted me, I just wanted out; and yet I was so tangled up with Mel, infatuated, adolescent with desire . . .

"Go and talk to the Splice," Mel said, dialling the jet up stronger still, "this is too good to waste. Unless you want to play . . . ?"

Another teasing twitch of the water towards me, and if she'd only not been teasing, if she'd simply turned it on me full blast . . .

But, again, no idea. Too young: she saw the vomit on the floor and none of the ambiguity, apparently none even of the lust that had me aching to join her even as I wanted to spurn her and her friend the doctor and everything they stood for.

Lacking the conviction to do either, I did what she told me instead, puzzled out the door-controls and left her to her showering.

"How's the stomach?"

Dr Corossa, eyeing me askance. Amused. Both.

"Under control, I think. Grim control. Thanks. Sorry . . ."

"Don't worry about it. Worse things are spilled in here, on a daily basis. I could give you something to quiet your insides, if you like."

"No, thanks. You've got nothing that could quiet my mind," either side of it, the nauseated or the yearning, "and that's what's chewing up my belly. Besides, I'm hang full of drugs already."

"Indeed. Why is that? Mel-2 said you were an artist, but I didn't understand."

No more did Mel, I thought. "The drugs help me to . . . associate, with the culture I'm observing."

"I'm sure that's true, but other artists don't necessarily feel the need."

I shrugged. "Art is individual. And other artists aren't working with full-immersion protocols. For me, the drugs are crucial. It's not all about the tech, but I couldn't make the work I do, if I didn't have that extra connectivity."

"I don't suppose I understand that either—"

"—No, I don't suppose you do; my kind of work has never reached far beyond its point of origin. Spatially, I mean. It's really only popular in my own home system—"

"—but it seemed to me that you were achieving plenty of connectivity with Mel-2. Until you threw up on her pretty shoes."

"I did not. And yes, I was—but I said, I'm drugged up."

"She's not. Nor need you have been." That was the doctor in her, a disapproving realist. I wanted to ask her what I'd asked Mel, the question she'd ducked, my proof that she was hiding something; but before I could frame it any better than *why do so many people want to sleep with her?* Dr Corossa had moved on. "At least, if all you needed for your art was normal interaction. That you can have here, sometimes even for free. Perhaps you should explain to me about your art and how you make it. Certainly if you're going to want more drugs before you leave us, you'd better do that. I'd be your best source, but I don't pass them out for recreation."

I was sure not, just as I was sure that people would ask regardless. Try to buy, and simply up the offer when she said no, not recognising principle when they met it. And go away baffled in the end, not understanding the principle even once they had been introduced.

Me, I knew it well. We were old friends and honest friends, which isn't always the same thing. On a dozen worlds, on a dozen dozen stations, I had struggled to explain my art to those who stood in a position to encourage it, or to make it possible, or else to prevent it.

I said, "If there's anything you need to do for your patient, do that first. This could take some time."

"He has what he needs. The gel-sheet soothes and nourishes his skin; there are other drugs at work in his blood. His mind is elsewhere. If it comes back, well, there is somnolence waiting in the gel-sheet too. If that's not enough, he will doubtless let us know, and then you may need to break off your narrative. Until then, though, you have my entire attention. If Mel-2 ever comes out of the shower, we'll send her off to run around until she's dry."

"What is it about horses and hoses? Or is it girls and showers?— No, never mind. Art. What I do. At least you use technology here, it's not like I'm talking into a void"—as I thought I would be up on the Row, trying to explain to Ro or Dolph—"but bear with me, this is never easy. I've no 3-D vid or anything like it, there's nothing to show; the whole point is to be there, interlaced with the artefact . . ."

Art, my art: I tried to tell her about my art.

I explained that even in a public gallery an individual must encounter my work privately, alone and apart, because all experience is individual also and cannot be shared, any more than personality can. Even what I do is a long, long way from sharing. What I do, I bring a record—no, a report, or else an interpretation, a personal view—of my experience to others, individually. What happens then is an interaction between us, between my work and the viewer. What they see—what they hear, what they taste, smell, feel—is their response to my response to what I have seen and heard and so forth. More, to what I've felt about it: what I have feared, what been awed by, what desired. How I've been seduced.

I told her about the mirror fields that encompass the artefact, because all art is about the self: the artist first, and then the viewer. Just as artists can only ever see themselves reflected in their own experience, so viewers can only see themselves in their reaction to it.

I told her about the artefact itself, the effector. About the witty engineering of it, no two ever the same; and yet how they always have the same complexity of purpose, to seem to share. The artefact—people have tried to call them arteffectors, but I despise clumsiness—is the bridge between me and the viewer, as the drugs are the bridge between me and my subject. In truth, I'm isolated on either side, disjunct, an island in the middle of the river, a stopping-point, no kind of bridge at all.

That doesn't matter. It's the art that counts.

I told her about the art. How I'd met it one time, farmboy adrift in the city, wandered into a gallery to get out of the rain; and there was an artefact and there was me, and I didn't understand it but suddenly I had flavours in my mouth and no name for them. Lights in my head that were the songstars of Ras Talomar as Kesteven had

97

seen them, or as he had chosen to portray them, or as the artefact he'd made conveyed his choices, or as my dim mind interpreted all of that; and I was seized, stolen, trapped and lost and gone.

She kept asking about the artefact, while I kept trying to talk about the art. Nothing new there, except:

"True art is body-art," she said, shaking her head. "What you are, what you make of yourself. What others make of you. How can you make art out of things?"

I don't, I'd been trying to say so: art happens in the mindspace, the two leaps from me to artefact, from artefact to viewer. It's all about interface, but all she could see was the object, all she could hear was the science.

In the end, I said, "It's no good. I'd have to show you. You could come back with me," to my own home system and welcome so, back among the Upshot, a heretic restored, "but I don't suppose . . . ?"

"No," she said, "I don't suppose so either. Leave my work, to look at yours? Mine is alive, my work is with people, I have responsibilities."

"And so is mine, and so do I. We're not so different, Doctor."

"No? Then call me Splice, as the kids do."

"If you tell me about your work, and why it's so important. And why you don't take advantage of it yourself."

"Oh, that's easy—I need to keep myself pure, if I'm to do good work for my clients. All my tools, my records, my software, everything's designed for human-normal bodies, hands and eyes and so forth. Brains, too. I don't need a raptor's thinking, that bird's-eye view of the world overlying mine."

That made sense, I supposed, a little. If you knew more about the process than I did, perhaps. But, "You could fling yourself into a younger body, at least." She looked, oh, fifty or thereabouts, by downsider standards. You rarely saw anyone with a body-age above thirty, among the Upshot. If we stopped moving long enough to accumulate the years, we wouldn't be Upshot any longer. "Be faster, sharper, fitter than you are; do better for your clients, feel better in yourself . . ."

She shook her head, as I'd been sure she would. She didn't need me to think of that. I was only curious why she didn't do it, or what excuse she'd have.

"I do well enough as I am," she said, no more than that. No reason, no excuse.

And then the shower-room door slid open and out came Mel, as naked as she ever could be and gleaming wet, little rivulets of water still running from her flanks and tail, as she rubbed at her hair with a towel; and I was spiked by a simple and immediate lust that I could barely recognise as anything my own. Even as a downside teenager with no prospect of a second chance at youth, I had surely never been this turbulent, this urgent . . .

"There are air dryers in there," the Splice said mildly.

"I like contact," Mel said. "Texture. And I like being damp."

"I like to keep water where it belongs, which is not on my surgery floor. If you drip on my patient—"

"—the drips will just run off the gel-sheet, and it won't matter a damn. I know. But don't fret, I'll stay over here, out of your way. I was just getting lonely," with a petulant little stamp of a hind hoof, and—oh, help me!—even that I found erotic.

"She means you should have stayed," the Splice said to me.

"Yes, I understood that. But we came to ask after him," a despairing nod towards the birdman, "maybe to help me understand a little more about what happens here, technically or otherwise; not to, to fool around in your shower."

"The Splice wouldn't mind."

"I would," I said bluntly. "It's not what I'm here for today, it's not what I came to the Row for; I'm not one of your bloody tourists, looking for exosex shocks to show to my drinking-mates back home."

"And yet . . . ?" the Splice prompted me, despite Mel's scowling.

"And yet. Exactly. And she's playing with me, playing with the way I feel, I mean, look at her"—knotting that towel below her armpits now, so that it hung like a damp curtain with all the promise and allure of concealment, and never mind how intimately I already knew what it ventured to conceal—"and I don't know why—"

"Only to distract you," Mel muttered, faux-resentful and utterly unconvincing, "to take your mind off your paranoia about that decant, try to help you have a good time while you're here, what's wrong with that?"

"—but it's more than that, it's both of you. You both know, don't you? You *know* how hot I am for Mel—"

"—Forgive me," the Splice murmured, "but it is a little obvious—"

"—which is one reason why I'm sure something abnormal's going on, because I'm not usually crude or obvious," or blundering about with a visible erection. "Nor so readily seducible, either, when I'm working; but I've been ready since I came to Rotten Row," even that first encounter with Tethys, if he'd wanted sex with me I had been ready, "and I think the two of you know why, and it's past time that you told me."

They looked at each other, and shrugged. At least, Mel shrugged and the doctor nodded. Mel took a breath and said, "That decant, all the human-normal ones made for tourists—"

Made and re-used, over and over; it hadn't slipped my mind, only—finally!—bypassed my stomach, apparently. I could think about it and not even want to vomit, even thinking about the uses this body had likely been put to already. There was no muscle-memory, no one in here now but me. Their whole practice of decants must be predicated on that. Our own policy of discards assumed it too, that nothing was left behind in the abandoned shell. Otherwise we were all murderers, unless we'd all been murdered.

Not that, then, not some acquired taint of random tourist lust. Mel seemed to have stranded herself, though. I said, "What about it?" and she didn't or couldn't respond; it was the doctor who went on for her.

"It may seem standard human, but it's not exactly Pure. Not unaltered, I mean. I'm sorry."

She was apologising for what was entirely out of her control, clearly, nothing to do with her and nothing she approved of; and she too still found it difficult to say clearly what she had to say, she needed another prompt.

"What is it, then, what have they done to me?"—though it wasn't done to me deliberately or specifically, I was just an ongoing victim, and I was pretty much ahead of them already; it wasn't so hard to work out, even from that bare admission. Take the fact on board, that this body had been gene-adjusted, and after that it only needed my symptoms to be interpreted. I could do that for myself, I had done it already. I just wanted to hear one of them say it aloud.

One or the other, but Mel surprised me with the sudden truth; I'd been looking to the doctor. "It's a hormone," she said, "that responds to morph pheromones. Tourists come looking for a thrill; we make sure that they get what they're looking for."

"They don't all want to get laid. Surely."

"No," the doctor said, "though you'd probably be surprised by the percentages. It's transgressive, simply to come to the Row. Not all illicit kicks are sexual, of course—though most of them are, at core—but those who come looking for something other, they mostly find their pleasure reinforced by a hormonal kick."

I could understand that, I could believe it, but I couldn't accept it. This wasn't a simple surge I was feeling. I'd played with my own hormonal balance for any number of reasons, any number of times. I knew that tingle in the blood, that sense of primacy shifting, becoming more primal. This was something else, something more. I told her so.

"Yes," the doctor said, "I'm sure of that. Even our most eager tourists aren't usually so priapic they need to complain about it. I think that cocktail of drugs you swallowed is exacerbating things. Extravagantly. I could give you a shot to counteract the hormone, but I don't know what that would do to your system as a whole, and I don't want to trigger another set of complications. Can you live with it? Now that you know?"

"Maybe. I'm not even sure that I'm staying. I need to work through this . . ."

"You need not to run away from it," Mel said. "Be angry if you want to; hell, be angry with me if you want to, I can take it. But like the Splice says, we're transgressive. You knew that, it's what you came for. You've found it, you're living it. How else are you going to make your art? If you quit now, you should quit forever. Be a roustabout, be a clerk, be anything you want but don't claim to be an artist if you walk out on the experience you were hungering after." And she gave me a good dramatic pause then, and then a smile, and then, "Take more cold showers. I'll help."

And then, in response to my expression or the doctor's snort of impatience—both, perhaps—she added, "I mean, I'll keep away from you. I'll leave you to it, hand you over, find you a guide you don't want to lay. Dolph'll do it. He's pure. Pure-born and human-normal, still in his first body. Not for want of saving up, but he still needs to grow some. There's nothing in him to trigger you. Or you could ask the Splice, if you can afford her . . . ?"

I'd like to spend more time with the doctor, but I didn't think she'd hire herself out as a guide. Also—whatever it was that was driving me, my intellect or my gonads or something else entirely—I didn't want to lose Mel. She was too useful. I told myself. Then I told her. "No, I need you: to tell me things, to find things, people, whatever. That hasn't changed. But I need you to be honest with me. No more holding back. Can you?"

"Oh, I can do that. My speciality."

"Good, then. In which case, I can . . . control my feelings."

"Or you could indulge them," she said. Suggested, with a glimmer of earlier Mel in the wisp of a smile that she gave me. "Either way. It does no harm, truly. It's only sex, you're only passing through. Both of us, we're only borrowing these bodies en route to somewhere else, so why fret what we do with them?"

I was full of insights this morning, though they came in slow succession. I said, "Mel? Do you have boosted hormones too?"

"Lord, yes. Carmel is a party girl; for her, this was a party body. Why wouldn't she want to have fun with it? But if she'd been dour and hadn't done that, I'd've asked the Splice to fix me up anyway. You know what I do; you know what I am. I'm here for the tourists. It helps, if I'm as keen as they are."

"Even knowing why, knowing what makes you so keen?"

"What difference does that make? You feel what you feel. If you feel hungry, you eat. You don't worry why you're feeling that way, whether it's a natural response or some kind of conditioning or a short-circuit somewhere between your belly and your head. Me, I feel hungry all the time, and maybe that's because I've got a great horse body with a belly I can't fill, or maybe it's because they gave me a grazer gene that tells me I'm hungry all the time, because they knew I'd have this great horse body to feed so I'd need to be always eating. It's all the same to me, I can't tell one from the other, I only know I'm hungry. If I ever feel full, it's because I've eaten three buck-etfuls of sprouts, plus all the supplements she forces down me, and none of that is any fun at all. Doesn't stop me enjoying the feel of it, being full." And then, when I was clearly unpersuaded, "Look. Everything about this body is artificial, in the sense you're thinking. It was designed, engineered, by someone not quite as smart as the Splice here but better funded and probably better equipped, in a lab a lot like this one only way up on the high side. What's natural, about a centaur? I've got plass in my *bones*, because some overpaid splicer thought it would be a good idea. Why would I worry about a few enhanced hormones pumping around in my blood? When they make my life easier, and a lot more fun? I've got the urges, and I go with them. Whether or not I'm getting paid. You could do the same, that's all I'm saying. Whether or not you get any benefit, any art out of it."

I shrugged a surrender, but only to the argument, not the prin-ciple. I didn't mean to sleep with her again, though I was aching to.

How long had it been since I'd felt so alien within my skin, so out of sorts with the body I was wearing? Not since my first nervous flings: perhaps not since my first time as a woman, learning newness and change from the inside out. Even then, it had been clear that the wrongness was my own, an unfamiliarity that bordered on the gauche, that could be addressed by learning. This time, the wrongness lay in the flesh that made my envelope. I could grow inured, perhaps, but nothing more than that.

Nor was I sure that I ought to. That swift return to NeoPenthe was still in my mind, a siren call. It was only that the call of the art was louder, unless it was those hormones deafening me, deadening me to any urge to leave.

I said, "If the Splice'll give me drugs, here and now, I'll stay."

Dr Corossa hissed, like a vessel under pressure. "I will not. I said already, I think you've had too many drugs already."

"I know you did, but you're wrong, demonstrably; I haven't had enough. You also said that you were my best chance of more. I need a boost, at least. If my regular regime was working, I wouldn't be throwing up when you tell me that this—decant—is just a little bit like Mel's. I wouldn't be having so much trouble with the concept that it's hard just to say the word. I should be starting to share by now, not still antagonist. Maybe I need different drugs; maybe I just need more. I don't know, we can talk about that. But I need something, or else I can't stay. There's no point my staying if I can't work, and this is not working for me."

It was so much not working, I was almost shaking with the tensions, the contradictions, the extreme discomforts of it: only keeping a tight grip on my body because if it broke into the stress-patterns it wanted to, that would be another reason for her to deny me drugs.

She wanted to deny me anyway, I thought—what did she care for my art, or my pleasures, or my neuroses?—but that Mel took her to one side and murmured at her for a minute. It's an operation, when a girl whose bulk of body is horse takes someone to one side; it can't be done subtly, and she didn't try.

It's good to have an advocate. Even so I was glad when the surgery door slid open, a distraction for all of us; gladder when I saw the extraordinary figure that came through, ducking his head when he didn't really need to, only that his crest was brushing the ceiling.

Tethys blinked a little at the sight of me—a briefly, weirdly human moment translocated into an alien face—and reached to close his fingers over Mel's as he glanced at the shrouded birdman, then finally met the Splice's gaze.

"Well?"

"Not well at all," he said, in that voice of his like untuned bells, resonant and harsh. "Word is, Promethea just got bored. Being halfway round, this close to the 'chute, she decided to put an early end to this performance. Her next big production isn't ready, so she's going to go Pure for a while, absolutely straight. She'll walk a lap as a normal human girl."

"What about the birdman?" It was what we were all thinking, but Mel was the one who asked.

"Ah, well, that's part of being Pure, apparently, when you're Promethea. She won't want exotic servants, she won't need a cast of elaborate morphs around her, so she sent them all away."

No great surprise in that, apparently. No doubt the wealthy did it all the time. But, "She could, she could at least have given him a body he could talk with, say what he wanted, find some other kind of work . . ."

"Yeah, but that's a part of being Promethea. Pure or otherwise. It'll add something to her legend, that she left him as she'd made him. She left them all that way, said it was the Pure thing to do. The Upshot way, she said."

No, not that. The Upshot would have flung them out of Rotten Row, into random bodies on NeoPenthe. And then let them come back if they chose to, naturally. That's the Upshot way: never to stand between anyone and their chosen damnation, and then to condemn them for their choices, absolutely.

"It's not exactly a surprise," Mel said, with a kind of depressed ferocity. "She was always such a shit. That's why she was prime candidate for—"

For what, she didn't say: stopped, rather, in that way that people do when they've stepped inadvertently over the edge. When they have suddenly no sense of ground, only a building awareness of how far, how very far there is to fall.

They all, all of them glanced at me, one wary instinct between the three of them, something like a signed confession. On a blank sheet, details to be filled in later.

Details to be filled in now. I said, "What? Prime candidate for what, Mel?" And when she hesitated, "Come on, tell me all your sins. I've thrown up already; you're too late to shock me now."

"Well, but—can I?"

She asked Tethys, who shrugged; it was the doctor who gave her a fuller answer, and that was brief enough.

"I see no reason why not. It was only ever an idle fantasy for idle children. Most revenge-conspiracies are. It's not criminal to dream."

"She would still have killed us all, if she'd heard about it." Mel was offended, to be so dismissed. It served as a reminder—as if I needed it—just how young she was.

"Oh, I didn't say it wasn't *dangerous*. Just ineffectual. You tell him about your plotting, if you like; I think you can trust him not to laugh."

She almost patted poor Mel on the head, though I noticed that she knew enough, she was wise enough not to pat her on the rump. Then she walked away.

Mel glowered after her. "She helped, she was right there with us when we were making plans . . ."

From what the doctor said, I didn't think that 'plans' was quite the word. Still, "What plans?" I said, amused and exasperated, suppressing both. "Tethys, are you going to tell me?"

"No, he's not. I am. If you promise not to throw up again."

"Promise. Breakfast all gone; nothing left to throw."

"Oh, are you hungry? I could—"

"Mel. Now, please. Tell me. What were you planning to do to Promethea?"

Mel took a breath and eyed me doubtfully, and said, "Steal her next decant, when she goes for the fling."

Then she waited for me to understand her.

It took a moment.

Steal Promethea's identity, she meant: take the fling in Promethea's stead, and claim to be her thereafter. A capital crime everywhere among the Upshot community, the sin that dare not even think its name.

There's the Upshot community, and then there's Rotten Row. They do things differently here.

She said, "It was really just for the money, when we were talking about it; we might have picked any of the highsiders. She was always favourite, though, just because she's so foul. Now—well, I wish we could've found a way to do it. I'd do it without the money, even, now. As a punishment. She deserves to lose everything she's got. And we had such a lovely plan to take it all away from her . . ."

She was pining for lost dreams, a hope already surrendered. I knew that wistfulness from long experience. Loss is a human constant, far more so nowadays than death is. The Upshot can keep a fling ahead of death—who knows how long? We haven't found the limits yet—but every fling is another measurement of loss, a surrender as much as a great leap forward.

I said, "How could it be possible?"

Not that it was; she'd said as much, they couldn't find a way to make it work. Even so, outside Rotten Row it couldn't even be considered. Here apparently it was at least worth talking about, or the doctor wouldn't have been involved.

The doctor was back, from her lab; I knew that when I felt the cold pressure of a hypo spray against my neck.

I twisted away, startled. "What was that?"

"The drugs you were asking for."

"I thought we were going to talk about that?"

"Did you?" She smiled blandly and went away again, before I could explain to her just how doctors behaved in a civilised society, how no one should ever be given a treatment—for sickness or for art, no difference—without careful discussion, what it was and what it did and what the costs might be.

There are civilised societies, and then there's Rotten Row.

I knew the bite of my drugs-of-choice, I knew the sense of them, the drift of me within them; I hadn't been spiked here, she'd given me what I asked for. And now she was coming back with bottles and glasses, some more welcome prescription. One for her and me, another for the two morphs—the two other morphs, I suppose I should say, but it was still too hard to line myself up beside them, all unwilling in my alteration.

The drink she shared with me was alcohol, but nothing stringent: dry and light, eminently fit for a midday conversation with friends. By their longsuffering look and the sweetly simple scent of it, the other two had fruit juice, soft and harmless, fit for children when they were let join the grown-ups.

She said, "You were asking how it would be possible, to steal another's identity? It's possible because this is Rotten Row, and everyone's an exhibitionist. You've taken drugs of assimilation, you know their effects and how effective they are. They would be crucial to the process. Mostly, though, it's possible because people just want to be looked at. Like everything on this station, height exaggerates; money feeds the impulse. Your pretty Mel-2 here, she's an amateur next to the highsiders. The average highsiders, they're all amateurs next to Promethea. She has it all recorded, broadcast, archived: not only her performances out on the Row, but her whole life, waking and sleeping. All her friends, all her business: everything has to be known, because how else could it be talked about?"

"We could have that archive," Mel said, "all of it. With that and the drugs, we could train someone to be Promethea, absolutely: under her skin, inside her head. Living her life. When you know everything about her life from the outside and everything about her character from the inside, what else is there?"

Individuality, identity, the undiscoverable: it's what Upshot law and art both seek to protect, that combination of personality and experience that cannot ever be replicated. She was too sanguine. Of course she was; she was young.

Also, though, she was right. It could be convincingly imitated. No one in that surgery, no one on that orbital knew it as well as I did, who had spent my creative life slipping out of my own skin to borrow others' feelings and then to pass them on.

The trouble, of course, lies in making the substitution. Where identity can be passed from one physical body to another, it takes careful management to be sure that anyone is who they say they are. In the Upshot community we have protocols, bureaucracy, paranoia; here on Rotten Row they had blunter and more exotic methods.

"When a highsider takes a fling, one side to the other, they just take over both 'chutes entirely," Tethys said. "Take them offline to anyone else, send everyone out except for one technician. They don't even trust their own people. Maybe they especially don't trust their own people. Those get to watch each other outside the door, with only the highsider and the tech inside. That's the physical security, that there just isn't anyone else let in."

"And you're the tech," I guessed.

"Sometimes, yes. For Promethea, always."

"She's paying for his decants," the Splice said. "She thinks she buys his loyalty with that. She's very stupid."

"She's mean," he said, as if that discounted his debt and justified betrayal. Perhaps it did. The birdman in his silence said it did.

"So what else is there?" I asked. That couldn't be the limit of her security, just a vacated chamber. Even here, that couldn't be enough.

"Once she's gone, after the fling, her people come back in to witness that I'm still there and the decant is empty; then they take that to the carboniser and destroy it. But before that, before she goes, last thing she does, she whispers a codeword to one of her morphs. He's another flyer, but he's got dragonfly wings, he's really fast. So she does that and away he goes, all the way round the Row to the Downchute. Then I send her. And her people greet her at the other end, and make her comfortable, and wait; and when he gets there, he tells them the word, and they ask her what it was. That's it."

It was simple, and childproof—and at least two of us weren't children. I could see two easy ways to break it, and only one of them required help on the inside, the subversion of one of her people. I said, "And how were you planning to defeat her security?"

"Oh, the codeword's easy," Mel said. "See, Tethys has bird-sharp hearing, and he's in there with Promethea and her messenger, he just hears it, however quiet she thinks she is."

Uh-huh. I glanced at the Splice, who had the grace to look a fraction embarrassed, even as she shrugged and said, "Power is heedless. Over time, heedless turns to careless." Over-engineered was her own phrase; and granted that Promethea was paying for it, even so, Tethys had no observable need for that degree of hearing. I thought she'd just been playing for its own sake. Unless she'd been redesigning him specifically for crime. I didn't know how long Tethys had been wearing that particular decant, or how long they'd been planning this.

Trying to plan it. There was, of course, still a hole in their concept. I said, "So how were you going to fling someone else, instead of Promethea? Out of an empty chamber?"

"That's the problem. It's not just the 'chute's own chamber, it's that whole reception floor. Her goons chase everybody out, then search the place. We can do everything else, we just couldn't work out how to slip someone past their scrutiny."

"Fly them in," I suggested blithely. "There's an open gallery on that level; anyone with wings could do it. Hell, get the birdman to do it, he'd be perfect. The instrument of his own revenge."

"The Splice says that he couldn't. Even if he could fly again, he'd never pull off the substitution. He'll be too much damaged inside, she says." Which meant that Mel had thought of it, proposed it. Even if she'd only done that to have it shot down. She went on, "It wouldn't work anyway, they have thought about the gallery. She may be stupid, but her guards aren't. They leave someone out there, till after the fling. All the doors are watched. That's why it doesn't work."

It was a feeble reason, I thought, to abandon a plan: something to seize on, rather, when their nerve failed. I said, "What were you planning to do with Promethea, meantime? While your substitute took her place," and presumably siphoned off all her money. They'd said, they planned this as a robbery.

"Keep her safe, in storage here. We can do that indefinitely, just the code of her, what the 'chute would have sent. She'd be fine. When we were ready, we'd give her back a body and let her start again. Her rich friends would help her. Probably. If they believed her, if she could persuade them. Our substitute would be long gone, safe in their own name again, so everyone would know that she'd gone missing. Maybe people would believe her."

Clearly she wasn't much bothered, either way. Why should she be? She'd have her money, and so would the Splice, Tethys, all her friends would have their share. And their revenge too, seeing cruelty punished and knowing they'd achieved something worth doing. Satisfaction all round.

Just to be sure, I said, "You can put Promethea into the 'chute, start the process, and then rip her code out before it actually gets sent?"

"Yes, absolutely. We wrote a shunt that Tethys can slip into the system on the day, to dump her signal onto a datachip."

"That's not supposed to be possible." Paranoia leads to sealed systems; Upchutes do one thing, uninterruptable. Supposedly.

"It is here. We had to strip out the original coding and rewrite it when this place was built, to address all the non-human elements in our decants; it's wide open now. People work on it all the time."

Right. This was Rotten Row. And Promethea thought she was safe, whispering code-words to an insect? She thought that was security?

I thought I wouldn't really want to go through their 'chute again, even if it had been the only way off-station. Security is consonant with paranoia; the one almost guarantees the other.

Almost.

I said, "So you could do that, shunt her code onto a chip without their realising, destroy her decant, send them away happy—and then send through your substitute."

"Ye-es—but it'd need to be done sharp. They'd notice if she didn't arrive for an hour after we supposedly sent her off from here, and they keep the 'chutes bolted down for at least that long. They're sure to compare timecodes, when she took the fling and when they caught her. It wouldn't matter if it was a couple of minutes later than the goons at this end thought—but it would have to be just a couple of minutes."

I nodded. "You said they take her decant and discard it. All of them?"

"Yes, they all witness each other; but you still couldn't get anyone through the doors, they'd notice that."

"How about the gallery? Once the guard has gone?"

"Well, yes. I suppose. But we haven't got a flyer."

"That doesn't matter," I said. "You've got me."

The Splice, I think, had known exactly how to get me. Why else would she have given way on the drugs, just as Mel started to expound her plot? They were taking advantage of me twice over.

Even so, I think—I hope!—that I would still have worked against all my worst instincts to refuse them, except that the birdman lurked in the corner of my eye, and my guilt was absolute. They didn't know it, but I had done this to him, absolutely. It wasn't boredom that made Promethea quit her grand parade and abandon all her servitors, no. That would be me and the vicious game I'd played with her, a night's destructive conversation, *prick prick*.

And not even the Splice could have known just what I had to offer, what a ready-made solution I was. She was playing an instinct, I fancy. Riding her luck.

She was lucky, they all were lucky, perhaps. All except me, perhaps. I was snared by those dual thongs of drugs and hormones; I was riding something else that was not luck at all, that beast called manifest guilt, and utterly unable to jump off.

I said, "Splice, what are Tethys' claws made of?"

"Bioplass, we call it."

Well, they would. I said, "The same as in Mel's bones?"

"An elaboration. Much harder. And yes, all right, that's over-engineering too; he doesn't need claws that sharp, but I was curious to see how far it would go. He's my test-subject."

"It scratches regular plass."

"It does," which wasn't supposed to be possible, wasn't even plausible, but I'd seen it.

"Can you make me a set of pitons, out of that? And the same for my hands, some kind of clawed gloves?"

"No," she said. "It's not made, it's grown. I can bond it into a strand of DNA; I can't manufacture it."

Mel was a dog with a bone. I'd offered her hope, and she wouldn't let go of it that easily. "Promethea—whatever name she's using, I mean, now she's Pure—she'll be walking a lap of the Row, Tethys says. That'll take time, she won't hurry. You can accelerate a decant, Splice, with whatever alterations he wants. Can't you?"

"Perhaps. Growing it, getting it to one 'chute and him to the other, getting a slot for the fling—it's all possible, but it would be just as possible to see it all go wrong."

And I didn't much want to take even one fling from one of their 'chutes, after all I'd been hearing; but I was snared, I'd have done it if they'd asked. If Mel had asked.

Happily, she didn't need to. The Splice turned to me, shrugging. More secrets. "These decants we give the tourists, they're not just pheromonally adjusted. They're . . . primed, I suppose, for other alterations on the fly. It's—well, no, not surprising, but surprisingly common for tourists to want to try some mild morphing while they're here. They can be flung into a full-blown decant if they want, but that comes expensive. What we can do instead, we can recode the DNA of the decant they have, give them a boost and let them feel it change. There is pain, but we can sell that to them as part of the experience, or else drug them out of it."

"What are you saying?"

"You know what I'm saying. I can give you claws. Why do you want claws?"

Because they'd scratch plass, of course. Why else?

"You recover fast," Mel said, holding my hands a little doubtfully, a step short of triumphant. "An hour ago you were puking your guts up at the thought of this decant being used before; now you're bespeaking claws for it," with a glance through to the lab, where the Splice was hard at work on the coding. Everything's immediate, it seems, on Rotten Row: my conversion, my enrolment, my commission.

It hadn't quite been my intention, any of it. "Shows how good the drugs are," I said, squeezing her fingers, meaning to say, to let her hear *it shows how good you are.* The guilt was my own, my secret, nor for sharing.

She knew what I meant, what she thought I meant, and smiled at it happily. I had to cloud her sunshine; I said, "Promethea's next decant—it won't have these hormones, will it?"

"I guess not. We don't know what she's planning next time out, but she's not exactly famous as a lover. Doesn't like to share the limelight."

Obviously, necessarily, that would mean an end to me and Mel. I looked at her. "I don't want to lose you."

She smiled, with that tang of bitterness and sorrow that goes hand in hand with poverty, with necessity. With life. "I know. Me neither. But that was going to happen anyway, with or without this. Without any of this, you'd have gone off to make your art, and I'd have lost you—and you wouldn't care, because you'd be back in a nice clean Pure body, no nasty hormones making you fancy a pony-girl—"

"—I'd still have the memories, of feeling just like this. Trust me, I'll care—"

"—and this way, you'll be off on the high side for a while, out of my reach. Whatever she calls herself next, whatever she does with herself, she's not going to take up with a second-use cabbie, so don't even think it. If those drugs are any good, they wouldn't let you. And then you'll be off, back into the network, and we'd lose each other anyway. You do have to go, so that we can let her out into a fresh decant; you need to be long gone before we do. You're the one she can cry imposter on. She won't know how it happened, if we're careful; she won't know about us. And we're not setting you up, there's no kind of justice that can follow you from here. But you can't stay, that really wouldn't be safe."

The Splice came back from her lab with another hypo spray.

"Not your last chance to duck out," she said, "but this would be a good one. What you're doing, what you're proposing to do is foolhardy and illegal, and my assistance comes against my better, my *much* better judgement. Your judgement doesn't count; there's a double hit against you, because you have those drugs in your system which predispose you to agree with the mood in the room, and because Mel's pheromones are totally overwhelming your hormones, so you'll want to do anything to please her. If you had any sense, if you had any strength of will, you'd refuse what I have here, despite it all. This isn't what you came for. Any questions?"

"Only one." My head was actually reeling now, but I could keep up this far. "If you're so opposed to what Mel's after, why are you prepared to go along with it? To the point of donating your expertise?"

"Everybody's venal," she said. "Plus, I'm as angry as she is. This gives me what I want, a clinic on the high side and the resources to do better work; and up there, maybe I can prevent abuses like this," with a neat gesture of her head to where the birdman lay swathed in his gel-sheet. "At heart, I suppose I agree with her. I disapprove totally, but that doesn't mean she's wrong. Just wrong-headed."

"Doctor," I said, "I like you. Give me your drugs."

"This isn't a drug. You'll see. And I told you, call me Splice. This isn't doctoring, it's stupid criminal conspiracy."

"I'll call you Splice," I said, "if you call this art."

Art is as art does. Sometimes, art needs to act transgressive or else it ends up tamed, authorised, ineffectual. It can transgress laws of taste and decency, of course; that's practically a given. It can transgress laws of nature, with a little help. Here they treated laws of purity with contempt, and were prepared more or less to call that art. Laws of property, laws of the person: why would they balk at those?

Why would I?

Even among the Upshot—who like to see themselves as a breed apart, a polity of consensus—even among us, wealth brings heedlessness. I've never been a revolutionary; I have become wealthy myself, by many definitions. I haven't seen myself turn heedless yet, but I have been willing to watch and document abuse and not much want to resist it. That again is art, my art: to reach under the skin but from a distance, to watch until I understand, not to seek to change.

Ordinarily, I've been willing. Ordinarily, that is my art. Even under the drugs, which are ordinary to me.

Here, nothing was ordinary. I was no longer ordinary to myself. This body I wore had been cultivated, to respond expressly to what Mel was; the drugs I'd taken were designed to tune me to her wavelength, to make me respond to whatever elevated her. Between the two—well, no, I was not ordinary. I was raging alongside her rage, at the same time as I twisted and ached to please her.

Even in her absence, all of that was true.

Dolph was the one I saw most, in the days that followed. Volunteer or conscript, he played runner for me, in and out of the Splice's clinic with all the latest news of Promethea's doings, broadcasts of her at play in her new Pure body: taking public lovers to private parties and recording it all, shamelessly exotic and shamelessly revelatory. Her life wasn't an instance for shame, apparently: lived apart in the exclusive splendour of the high side but then scattered to the solar winds, as far into the network as she could send it before the clear precision of her tale disintegrated into rumour, innuendo, repulsion. To me on my home world, far-flung from the source, all the stories of Rotten Row had been one story, degradation and disgrace.

Every artist knows, you have to get close to see the detail, and then you can't see the work at all.

I was so close now, there was only the one detail I could see: Promethea, in all her festering glory. Other modmeisters were only significant where and how their lives and work touched hers. That might be often and fleetingly, it might be rarely, deeply; the Row was big enough—long enough, I suppose, where it's the circumference that matters—to allow cliques and cults, feuds and fetishes, genuine friendships and lifelong hatreds, such as you might find in any aristocracy.

I had to absorb all that. I needed the knowledge at my fingers' ends—or no, somewhere other than that, somewhere more stable and less corrupt, because my fingers' ends and my toes too were what kept me in the clinic while Mel was off and away all day, why the boy Dolph had to run my errands for me.

I had to commit Promethea to memory, her entire lifestory, her whims and lusts and terrors; and I had to commit a far more personal offence. Identity theft is the capital crime but body morphing is the sin that underlies it, or else the science that leads inevitably to it. Both.

They're skilled people, the gene-splicers of Rotten Row. They can make the subtle software changes, the hormones and phero-mones; they can grow their freak bodies, the surreal and impossible. Between those two, they can work any number of small and imme-diate miracles. If he's primed for it, they can slip a man a virus that will infect his DNA there and then, to change the way his nails grow.

I stayed in the clinic because she gave me claws, the doctor did.

Retractable claws.

For the record: it hurts, yes. A lot. Medicating the pain was complicated, both by the drugs I was on already and the effects, the demands of those drugs. They drive me to share, to feel, to experi-ence; which meant they drove me away from anything that numbed or veiled or stood as any barrier between me and the common truths of Rotten Row. I found myself pulling away from her proffered analgesics before I'd had time to say "yes please".

I told myself, over and over, that it was no more legitimately an instinct than the revulsion I felt as I watched my fingers, watched them swell and stretch and darken. The one feeling was borrowed and the other was learned, they were both entirely artificial; the only truth was pain, and that could be taken away. Sometimes. When I tried to sleep and failed monumentally; when my restless suffering disturbed the birdman too, the Splice would insist and I would yield to her hard-edged relief, like a steel curtain drawn between me and my own sensations.

The birdman's sufferings I was tuned to also, more diffusely.

Recovery is also change, it never brings you back to where you started. She said he'd never fly again, in that body.

I said, "Can't you do to him what you've done to me, remake him, grow him new wings?"

"No. Tourist bodies are primed for alterations on the fly, but only minor ones; regular morphs don't have even that much flexibility, any more than a Pure body does. Given access, I'd put him through the 'chutes, give him a Pure body for a while and let him tell us what he wants; this one I'd just discard. You'd approve of that."

But she didn't have access. Promethea had forbidden him that road. He and all her former servants were banned from the 'chute until she decreed otherwise, until she had at least completed her own Pure pilgrimage. All the Splice could do was heal him as best as might be managed: with ruined flesh and twisted tendons, everything askew, no flying now.

I might have tried to buy her the access that she wanted, entered a bidding-war if necessary, but that I was too caught up with villainy, with stealing that same access from Promethea. The state I was in, I couldn't have reached my own funds anyway, I couldn't have asserted my own identity long enough to claim them. Pain inhibited me, Mel infected me, Promethea infested me; in too many ways to count, I was literally not myself. Birdman would simply have to wait and suffer as I did, as we all did. His time would come. He was our oath, our binding, all we had in common.

I knew otherwise why I was doing this, because I was snared in a chemical confusion. I knew why Mel was doing it, apart from her drive for justice and revenge; she was doing it for the money. The same I guessed was true too of Tethys, although we never saw him, he was careful not to come. How much Dolph was involved, how much he knew I wasn't clear, but he was all boy: he'd do a lot simply for the adventure of it, never mind justice, and he'd do anything for Mel. Or for money.

I didn't know why the Splice was doing this, why she was allowing it, why a doctor would be involved in crime. Beyond that urge to see some reparation made, which in the rest of us at least was not enough; and the urge to wealth, which she had already admitted, but which in her I thought was still not enough.

So I asked her.

For fear of seeing me lost altogether in another's personality, she had me schedule hours where I wasn't listening to Promethea's voice, where I wasn't watching her walk or scanning her long, long history on the Row. To ensure that I kept to those schedules, she came to enforce them: to sit with me, talk to me, have me talk to her in my own voice, my own manner, of my own concerns.

So I asked her, why she was here and why she would do this.

She said, "I'm here because I came. One fling, once; and that trapped me, I can't leave now. Happily, I don't want to. My work, my life is here. And I would do this because—well, because this too is my work, unless it's my life."

She left me then, to check the birdman. He was unwrapped from his gel-sheet now, and conscious, which was the worse option of the two. Mute entirely, of damage or despair, he couldn't even shriek; he only lay burned and broken on his slab, his beak gaping for I knew not what, some coup-de-grâce perhaps but he couldn't say, he couldn't ask for it. I had the talons now, or would have soon, but he would need to ask.

The Splice felt the same, I thought. I was almost sure. She had blades for a swift end, drugs for a peaceful one, and she could give him neither without his express consent. Even if he had a voice, I wasn't sure that he'd have sense enough, sanity enough to use it; and of course that was another tool that she had and couldn't use, that gift of voice. There was a chill at the heart of her work, an ancient morality that prescribed all her actions, that proscribed any choices of her own.

That same morality, perhaps, was what brought her back to me; she wouldn't use one patient as an excuse to escape another. I said, "Wait, we need to—I need to take these one at a time. One fling? One? And you came here? That means . . ."

"Yes," she said. "I was born on NeoPenthe. Ridiculous name, ridiculous planet. Proximity heightens that native Upshot paranoia, to the point of immobility. Literal immobility, in the network sense: few of us ever leave NP, the Upshot find us poor ground for recruiting. We're so terrified of taint by association, we grow up terrified of the 'chute, the concept of discards, the whole idea of leaving one body behind and being uploaded into another. Add that the new body has been grown for us via a biotechnical process, which is so close to what they do on Rotten Row, so perilously close to sin . . . Well, it's no wonder that most of us flinch away and stay right where we were born, thank you, in the bodies we were born with."

"Not you, though . . . ?"

"Not me, no. I had the misfortune to be a scientist first and then a doctor, to see the advantages of gene therapy and want to override the laws. We had laws, on NeoPenthe: your genetic inheritance was inalienable, absolute. If you were sick to death, so be it. We couldn't be anything but Pure. I understood it, even when I was young; perhaps I even agreed with it, for us. In our particular circumstances.

"For me, though—well, in the end, I had to follow my heart. I wanted to learn about gene splicing, manipulation, everything. If I couldn't cure my own people, at least I could cure others. And if I wanted to learn so much, where better than here, on Rotten Row, where the specialists are . . . ?

"So I took the fling, and I came; and now I can never leave."

"No, you said that—but why not? Because of your clients, is it, Mel and Tethys and, and the birdman here, and all the rest of them . . . ?"

"No," she said, smiling thinly, "not because of them. They only want to stop me leaving. In fact, I stop myself."

"How so?"

"I'm afraid. I went through it once, that fling of yours, I left one body and woke up in another; and I couldn't bear it in that moment, and I wouldn't bear it now except that I must, it's all I've got. I'll never, never do that again. They're right, back on sweet NeoPenthe; it is an appalling, irreverent, ultimately transgressive act. I've spend half a lifetime—a human-normal lifetime, that is, which is all I want now—regretting it, and wanting my old body back. And of course I can't have that, it was destroyed the moment I'd left it. Not like this place, where it would have gone into the tourist tanks and been worn and worn again, a few days at a time, over and over. But—yes, I took the fling once, and I daren't face it again. Once was dreadful enough. I've grown accustomed, I suppose, to this body now, as I suppose you'd grow accustomed to those claws I've given you, if you spent time enough with them; I still detest it, and I always will. I look down and see hands that are not my own, moving to my instruction; I see a stranger in every chance reflection of my face. It doesn't jar me now, the way it did, but I'll never accept it, I'll never see myself within that face. To do it again, to go elsewhere and face all this another time, another body, would be—no. Unthinkable."

I wondered if she'd been born male, if it had been a gender-swap that had so overthrown her. I knew cultures where that would go almost without saying, where they had entirely refused a 'chute for precisely that reason, that they couldn't insist on being flung into discards of the same sex and couldn't abide the thought of change. I also knew cultures that simply wouldn't understand the difficulty. For me—for most of us, I think—it had been a nervousness, a thrill, an extension of adolescent discovery; over time it became almost routine. If I had a preferred sex, it didn't come to mind.

There was always another way to leave. Nothing material could ever come through a 'chute; however much they subsisted and recy-cled on the Row, there would be traffic, ships coming and going. She could beg or buy a ride off-station. Perhaps she had other neuroses, though. Months or years of coldsleep might play badly with her, if she was this uncomfortable already in her body. Never mind; I could allow her that much privacy, not to pursue her patent distress further. Besides, her pain hurt me.

I said, "Let's not think about it, then. You came here, and you made a life for yourself, you made a better life for others"—which was another way of saying *see how deep your drugs have reached inside me*, that I allowed that without thinking, that her work was an act of goodness—"but I still don't see why any of that would let you involve yourself with Mel and her mad plans?"

"I think it was Tethys' plan," she said, "more than it was Mel's. Mel was happy enough, until he stirred her up; he's the malcontent. But they are my work. At least, Tethys is entirely, and Mel will be soon. I didn't make her current decant, but her next will be mine. And her mind, her soul is mine already."

She shrugged against the weight of that, and went on, "I suppose you're thinking me maternal, these are my children and must be defended; but it's not like that at all. These are my *work* and must be allowed to work it out, all the permutations, all the consequences of what I do to them. Does that make them aggressive, transgressive, criminal? Greedy? Perhaps it does, perhaps that's what I do. Perhaps the morphing of their bodies morphs their minds to match. I don't know. None of us knows, I think—and it's important. I follow my work, I facilitate my work; I cooperate with their ambitions, their grand designs, because that is a part of my work. That's all."

"Not because you love them, then?"

"I'm lucky," she said, in flat contradiction of what she'd said before. "I love my work."

I'm an artist, is what she was saying; she'd said it before. Art implies everything that results. Actions have consequences, and art is always active. I know.

I knew. My art, my action was all turned on myself. Sometimes, it seemed, so was theirs turned on me. Mel came rarely, but now it hardly seemed to matter. When she was there I could be that passion, that hunger, I could shiver in my need of her and chase her dragon soul relentlessly, try to worm my way under her skin, the dual skins of her, horse and human, try to understand what made her so very much one person. And she had her own needs, her own passions; we could manage for a while to forget that she was so very much one person, and so independent of me.

When she wasn't there, I could mostly be Promethea. Her utmost fan, at least, her ultimate student. I stalked her, by every way there was. All the media were mine to chase her down, and there were media in me to absorb her. She had no escape, and nor did I. I could be the man who hunted her, or I could be the love-slave of the centaur; I could never be myself, except that I was the artist and this is what I did, this was my art. Made manifest, made me.

Promethea, when she was Icarine—and oh, shall we, shall we find an irony in that?—soaring on feathered arms, boned far too lightly for the human body she seemed to have: rising to the height of the light-bar, casting her shadow over a full degree of arc—it would be claimed later, though science would dispute that—and then losing all those feathers in a slow rain, see how they fall and scatter while she does not, while she hovers, waiting till they have come to ground to make her point. And then, when the evidence is there in people's hands and every tourist eye is gaping upward, then she makes her plummet.

Down and down, straight down, she ought to be shrieking; perhaps she is, perhaps she outfalls her own shriek. Down like a falling rock, down like catastrophe she goes—and no, this isn't irony. Irony is the birdman's work, selfconscious, self-aware; that must have been deliberate. This is just Rotten Row, the essence of it, what it's for.

Down and down, and where she hits, she splashes. Icarus must always fall into the sea. So she plunges, deep and deep, unwing'd by her falling; and her sea is a tall tall tank of water drawn in procession by her favourite morphs, and its walls are clear plass so that everyone can see how she plunges, how she becomes a creature of the sea, how she has gills to breathe and the webbing that was her wings serves now to propel her through the water, powerful in mastery, a whole new ending to the legend.

And she breathes and swims, and waves through the waves of her own motion, and is drawn away to some high and private residence where she will rest and play with her retinue and friends until her feathers grow back and the whole adventure can be lived through again . . .

Promethea, now that she is Pure: so Pure that she has forsaken names, making a virtue of her gender-choice by asserting that to be female is the Pure alternative, being homogametic, double-X; XY being inherently complex, unsimple, imPure.

She still leads her progressive life, every day a few degrees of arc; but now she walks, barefoot in the simplest robes, too light to be white samite. Those who go with her are her regular entourage, but they too have been inveigled or compelled into Pure human-normal decants, less even than the sexually-enhanced bodies of the tourists who gaze at them almost with dismissal. She makes it known that none of her companions is being paid for their presence. She is on pilgrimage, one lap of Purity, and as far as she's concerned she goes alone. If they choose to walk beside her, that is theirs to decide and theirs only.

She stays each night on the high side, of course, with one of her wealthy friends. Those who go with her must make their own arrangements, so she says. If they end up sleeping in the same great houses as herself, like bodyguards in rooms to either side of hers—as though they occupied official positions in her life, as they have done these last years, as no doubt they hope to do when this parade is over and her new decant brings new complications—then so be it. She has neither asked nor ordered it; she is not concerned what other people think. She is above such troubles now. She has become Pure.

She sees no evil, hears none, speaks none. She speaks little of any sort, listens to no one, watches the world with a hermit's distance even when it rubs right up against her, in her face, the great parade of Rotten Row that she has disdained, that she has rejected, that she is still more than ever a part of, even as she holds herself apart . . .

Once my hands and feet were healed—no, not healed; they were never harmed; but once they had stopped hurting—I moved out

125

of the clinic and back to Ro's. It was easier for Dolph to bring me what I needed, easier for the Splice not to have me underfoot, easier for me not to see the birdman always in the corners of my sight. He was recovering, mobile now, but that was worse. He had lost almost everything in Promethea's service, all but the power of flight. That he had thrown away himself, but his ugly awkwardness was a constant accusation against us all. He blamed her, for stealing his freedom and discarding his life so casually; he blamed himself, for the failure of that spectacular suicide dive; he blamed us, for saving what little there was left of him.

I thought. I thought that was what happened, in the unique privacy of his head. I couldn't know, but the drugs gave me better access than anyone else. I might have done better, only that he was not my focus. I was halfway to being Promethea, and when I looked at him I one-half saw what she saw, someone to be quite disregarded, trash to be dismissed as Purity demanded. No, she would not contribute to his further degradation; that would only involve her, bring her down. As he was, so let him be . . .

That was hard, for what there was left of myself. I was glad to be away.

And glad to see more of Mel, most of Mel, in her stable stall most nights: ridiculously, pathetically glad. Enraptured, but I knew that, she had spelled out the spell herself. As well she might, because she too fell beneath it, her own hormones in harmony with mine.

I did ask her once, if she didn't miss stallion sex. She pulled a face and said, "Yes. Hell, yes. But there are compensations."

And so there we were, a slow conspiracy, compensating each other and building to a climax long delayed, never ready for it until the day we must be.

The day that Dolph came running in to find us. Both together, as luck would have it, if you can call that lucky. Mel had taken a day off from the cab, so I had taken a day off from the study, infatuation, ingraining of Promethea. I had meant, I had thought to spend the whole day studying my other infatuation, switching from the one to the other woman, ingraining Mel so that I could at least take her with me when I went.

But Dolph came running in to find us and everything changed, everything was happening, was now.

He said, "Birdie—" with the last of his air, and could only stand there gasping, sweating, letting us understand calamity until he had breath enough to try again.

"You gotta come," he said, "Birdie's—" and this time it wasn't his air he lost, it was his words; he simply didn't know how to tell us something so momentous, though he was desperate to do it. His hands sketched vague and dreadful shapes in the air.

It took Mel longer to get onto her feet, having four legs to coordinate; by the time she'd done it, I was up and pressing a cup of water into Dolph's hands.

"Here. Drink, cool down, just tell us what he's done."

"And don't call him Birdie," Mel said, the mock-disciplinarian, frowning mightily.

Dolph ignored her, swallowed water, spilling some around the edges of the cup, the edges of his mouth; he said, "She was, She was doing her thing, you know, walkabout—"

"Yes," I said. *She* was always the woman who had been Promethea; in her current incarnation, she had no name to call her by. "We know. What happened?"

"Birdie got away from the clinic, while the Splice had the door open. He just ran out, she couldn't stop him . . ."

"She probably wouldn't have tried, Dolph. She has no right to hold him there. If he's well enough to get around, that's good. If he wants to go off on his own, that's his choice."

Besides, I wouldn't say this to the boy for the sake of keeping the lesson clean, but we could always find him again. Rotten Row was the most contained environment I knew, the end of the line. As was the birdman, contained in that mute and awkward body, flightless now.

For a brief inconsequential moment I thought this must be the crisis, that the birdman had run off; but, "The Splice says he must've been listening while we planned, while you guys talked about the plan, about what She was doing, how far She'd got . . ."

"Dolph." Mel was suddenly imperative, there beside me and taking his hands, holding them hard. "What's he *done?*"

"He caught up with her, out on the Row. I don't know who was with her, but he got by them, and he—he *hurt* her. You know? That beak he has, those claws, he really ripped her up. He ate her liver, I think. That's what they say. None of us saw it, but . . ."

But he'd picked up the talk on the streets, and this was a distillation; and his natural adolescent passion for drama was warring with his anxiety for the plan, he wanted both to build it up and play it down simultaneously. It's hard to be young.

Harder to be the birdman's victim, though, just now. We'd been planning our own vengeance, but not upon her body. And not like this: abrupt, unthought-out, lethal . . .

"How is She," though it was fairly easy to guess, and to guess the boy's urgency alongside, "have you heard?"

"Don't know. Not dead, I guess, because they're bringing her straight to the 'chute, as fast as they can move her. They've taken the 'chute offline already, the whole system's closed down. Her goons are on the doors and no one's been let stay inside, except for Tethys."

Our plan was—had been—dependent on good intelligence and time, time above all. No plan survives first encounter; now it was all dash and panic and improvisation.

"What about the birdman," I did—just—have time to ask, "what's the word on him?" For sure, he couldn't have escaped capture. If he'd tried. It was only whether they'd killed him in his moment there, all the slow pain of his survival thrown away in another frantic, desperate choice.

"They're holding him," Dolph said, with a fatalistic shrug. "For her, for when she's settled in a new decant. She'll decide what's to be done with him then."

There would be time enough, cruelty enough done to him before then, I guessed; but that was the nature of justice on Rotten Row, in a habitat without a hi-hal or any system of police. It lay in the hands of the wealthy, to turn against those that injured them; the poor policed each other. It wasn't unusual to work freelance against one who had injured you or yours. The only striking aspect of Mel's conspiracy was that it turned against a highsider, who should have been far out of the reach of her ambition.

Mel has plass in her bones. She might seem scrawny, but she could take my weight. I was astride and we were off, leaving Dolph to trot behind as best he could, not fast enough.

The quickest way around the Row in daylight is not the Row itself, the great parade, all that weaving and dodging other folk and every-one's attention. It's quicker to use the back alleys and market lanes that parallel the highway.

So Mel taught me, that day. I clung to her back—and it was not, so not anything like riding a horse, or any beast of transport; I had my arms wrapped tight around her waist, as though I rode pillion on a slipbike, while my legs tried to clamp similarly around her working ribs, her other ribs, horse-ribs—while she put her head down and charged. Arms flailing, slim shoulders barging the slow and the stupid out of our way with all the weight of her horse-body behind them; hooves skittering and sparking, she made a hero's dash of it, a hellride that should have been sung for generations, except that this was Rotten Row and it didn't seem to be so unusual. I heard curses shrieked at our backs, where a kicking leg had upset a barrow of fruit or a bruising impact knocked some dawdler off their feet, but mostly people heard us coming and squeezed out of the way; mostly they snatched their produce to safety or else Mel ducked around it with a swerve like a spooked colt; mostly we came through the narrow alleys with remarkably little fuss, remarkably little damage left behind.

Even so it was a hard ride, a hot ride. Mel sweated; I had trouble holding on, as she alternately jinked and hurtled. And not even she could keep up that pace all the way back to the 'chute. Before the arch of it came in sight down the rising curve of the horizon, she'd slowed to a walk; before we reached it, I was down from her back and walking with her, hand in hand.

Back in the alleys there, the arch was a rising artefact, a leaping thrust of plass. Its strength was visible in its muscle engineering; these blocks and girders were the footings for the 'chute's great spire, and not shy to show it.

Standing square-on as they did to the light-bar, their hind faces stood in shadow. We walked to the rear of one vast rising girder, almost a vertical face, its plass surface cool and flawless with that soft semi-transparence that belies a crystal hardness.

Palm to palm, Mel and I looked at it, followed it upwards, up and up. Then we looked at each other.

"Keep faith," she said quietly.

"Always," I said, and meant it; even after the impetus was gone, even when I was in another body, I would do that so long as I could hang on to the least semblance of myself. Art is about honesty if it is about anything at all; I would keep my word when I had no reason left to do it, simply because keeping my word is what I do.

I kissed her, inhaled the hot smells of her one last time—giving myself deliberately one last dose of her, one kick of a reason to do this now—and then I turned away, to face that climbing girder.

And turned back in startling, seismic doubt, because I had never had the chance to climb in this body, barely any chance to prepare it for the climb; and sometimes fear throws up ideas, desperation can be practical at heart. I said, "Mel, wait. I know there's no hi-hal here," no governing artificial intelligence, "so who controls the station, the rate of spin, the traffic, all of that?"

"There's an office," she said vaguely, bewildered. "People work there . . ."

"People you know?"

"Of course." It was a point of pride with her, that she knew everyone. Everyone who worked, at least. Not the highsiders, but the people who made the Row function, who kept the wheels turning.

"Run and talk to them. Bribe them, inveigle them, do anything you need to do, if you can only get them to reduce the spin for the next hour. Just to give me a lift, let me not hang so heavy. Just five per cent, people won't even notice, they'll only feel that little bit fitter, ready for anything," but it could make all the difference to me.

She shrugged, even while she was nodding: "Oh, we do that all the time. Highsiders pay for it, when the kids are trying out their wings. No trouble. Don't wait, though, you can't afford to wait . . ."

I promised not to wait. And kissed her again, turned again, didn't even wait to see her canter away.

Kicked my soft shoes off and flexed fingers and toes, felt the claws the Splice had given me slide out of their protective sheaths.

The sheaths were to protect me and those about me, not the claws; there was nothing here on this orbital that could chip or blunt their edges.

Plass is traditionally, proverbially the hardest substance we can make—but Tethys' claws could scratch plass, when he was in a temper. Not made but grown, organically engineered, bioplass is harder than hard, sharper than sharp. Which in practice means harder than a sheet of plass, sharper than a plass blade and even longer-lasting.

Which, put to use, meant this: that a man remade with the Splice's claws could stand before a monstrous, inviolable girder, reach out and scratch it lightly, see how the plass curled away like paint beneath his nail, eternal crystal ripped to a shred.

He could set one hand against it with the fingers spread wide and feel five claws dig in, feel what a grip they gave him.

He could stretch the other hand higher and grip, and hang from it while he drew his legs up, so; and then his feet came into play, long and prehensile toes with their own claws biting, taking his weight like living pitons . . .

Hand over hand and one foot after the other, I climbed that girder in its own shadow, where no one was likely to see me.

Soon enough, too soon I was sweating as Mel had. The Splice had enhanced my strength and stamina beyond human-normal, plenty enough—she said—to make this climb, but my muscles ached regardless. I hoped it was only lack of work, unreadiness. I climbed for recreation, usually with friends, but ordinarily I'd give weeks of preparation to a serious climb. And have my discard fit, life-fit before I started training, not just barely out of the tank . . .

The worry, of course, was that this decant was not only unfit, it was unready on any level, half-made. Two more weeks, the Splice's changes needed, to mature in my flesh. The higher I climbed, the harder the fall dragged at me. I kept my face to the wall and never looked down, and felt it none the less; the emptiness below had a sucking, summoning quality.

I climbed, and my joints burned even before that handy girder met and melded with others, curving over to become the underside of the arch, the base that the 'chute was set upon: leaving me hanging upside down like an insect clinging to a ceiling, my claws biting deep into the plass.

Too deep: I was wasting effort, overworking. And still not going to slack, not for a moment. I couldn't do it relaxedly, taking just the nip I needed to give my claws a hold; I drove them in and clung fiercely, with all the strength that I could bring to that good work.

And felt the gradual change when it came, as my hanging weight grew less than it had been, the station slowing in its spin. That relief wouldn't last, I knew. I swung myself along, limb by cautious limb, as swiftly as I dared. Anyone gazing up this high would be gazing more or less directly into the light-bar's glare, and ought not to pick me out beyond it. Nevertheless, I was glad to reach the peak of the arch, where I could swing myself onto a vertical face again and scramble up into that angle where the observation-gallery jutted out from reception.

Here I just had to sink claws deep and hang there. I was safe enough, so long as I could just hold on. Above me, I could just make out a dark smudge through the semitransparent plass of the gallery floor: a smudge that moved, as the man that made it paced to and fro. He was watching for intruders, for thieves, for me.

Watching the sky, of course, rather than the impossible climb below his feet; and not in all likelihood watching with any great attention, because why would he, when he must know what a waste of time this duty was? He and his predecessors had stood this guard year after year, unchallenged, inviolable. They were known to do it; so long as that held true, their simple presence was discouragement enough. They were watched; which being true, they didn't need to watch. Like everything on Rotten Row, it was all about being seen . . .

Which he was, and I wasn't. I hoped I wasn't. I hung there with a failing strength and a looming sense of catastrophe, a building pain in my fingers, in my toes; and thought that if I could see him, looking up, he could equally well see me if he chanced to look down.

Almost, I wanted him to do that.

Almost, I wanted to pull myself over the gallery railing and confess, rather than hang there another minute while my own weight pulled my nails out: these grand claws that were so useful and so not-quite-ready, immature, vulnerable.

It's a famous torture, pliers, nails.

It might have been five per cent easier than otherwise; I might have muscles amplified beyond human-normal.

Even so. Famously, it's a torture. And in the end, famously, everyone gives in to torture, everybody—every body—breaks; but, famously, if you survived this long you can survive another minute, and another, if it's only getting marginally worse. One increment at a time, you can hang on.

I hung on.

At last, a voice called the man inside.

He went, I hung. Then there was another blur of form above, more strangely shaped, widespread feet and a voice that summoned me like bells.

I clambered painfully up and over the rail, stood there dropping blood on the plass of the floor.

What I wanted, I wanted nothing more than to sink down with my back to a wall, smear that blood, shiver and breathe for a while. But we only had a brief window here, strictly limited time. Pain is only pain; like bodies, it goes away. It didn't matter, it couldn't matter. Once a body is discarded, what can it possibly matter, what that body endured before?

"Where is she?"

Tethys tapped his beak, where the Splice had made him a little pocket, just enough to hold a datachip.

I'd meant *where's her discard?*, but I knew the answer to that too—down the hall, behind a door, where it was being reduced to a disc of carbon, witnessed by her men. My own would follow, once the men were gone. No useful decant for the tourists now, it was only evidence to be destroyed. That and damaged goods, distorted, broken. Bleeding.

Much more importantly, "I didn't see a flyer?"

"No, it didn't get here before they had to fling her. She was unconscious already, there'd have been no codeword anyway. When the flyer arrives, that's the message it'll have to carry."

Which was code enough, and all I needed to know.

We'd won already, the system was a gift. It was inherent: the Upchute's isolation, its height and inaccessibility, its attested emptiness guaranteed that she went in alone, so whoever came out at the Downchute end was her by definition, once it was confirmed not to be the technician who had sent her.

Tethys flung me through, and I had that hit of disorientation, rising and stumbling out into the reverent welcome of people I didn't know; but a woman with fur, with furred ears and tail stepped forward from the throng and said, "Lady, welcome to your new revelation," and this was her decant ritual, I knew, I had seen it played out more times than I could count. There was a formula, for their comfort as much as their mistress's. More than. I knew whom I should speak to, and in what order; whom I should ignore; what I should say, what not say, what do and not do to reassure them all.

And I did none of that, because it was futile as a security protocol, because if I could learn it so easily then so could anyone, drugs or no drugs; but because I'd had the drugs, because I'd had her in my head all these days, because I *knew* what she would do, I broke that ritual apart.

I gazed down at myself, my body, naked and female and perfect, young; and I said, "What kack is this?"

"Lady . . ."

"What have you *done* to me? Where is my proper decant? Where is my *dragon* . . . ?"

That was her next project, the whole Row knew it; plans and specs and animations had been leaked, perhaps deliberately, while she made her Pure pilgrimage, just to keep her fans interested. And here she was in a human-normal shell, unadorned. Even fresh from the fling, unsteady on unfamiliar feet, unable even to recognise herself, she would be raging.

So I did that, I raged; and felt the fury of it very genuinely, as I felt their nervousness in the face of it, as I felt their brief relief that yes, this was indeed their mistress safe restored to them.

Which was their plea, "Lady, the dragon is not here, not ready. You know it's not. Nor any of your own spare decants, we had no time, for your own life's sake we had to hurry . . ."

"So what is this you've put me in? Give me a mirror, hurry . . ."

One of the men had a pocket-glass that threw a reflective field on the wall. I looked, I saw, it only fed my anger. "This is a tourist-decant. Isn't it?"

"Lady, be calm . . . !"

"You put me in a stinking *rental*, and you tell me to be calm?" She had her reasons, I had mine; we both felt like throwing up.

"Lady, you're just out of the 'chute, it's not good to be so agitated. You needn't keep this long, only till your dragon's ready—"

"I needn't keep you long. Any of you. I own you all, I own your *decants*, or do you forget that? You think you can control me, slam me into whatever weak little body you choose . . . ?"

And so on, and on: a tantrum backed by tears, while they brought me clothes, while they took me to a private rear entrance of the Downchute, while I stung each of them with their own names and fragments of their history, all in the guise of threats. Temper was a fine disguise to see me through the unfamiliar ways of this heretical 'chute and out into the high side, where I was still a stranger.

A carriage, drawn by her favoured centaur-men; a long ride, up a helical ramp and along a quiet private road, nothing but contrast to the hurly of the Row below. The hurly of her anger might have been nothing but contrast to the cool grim calculations of my mind, except that I was calculating nothing now, only seizing the easy shelter of that tantrum. She was my place to hide, and I went to ground in her.

Went to ground, and stayed there. She has her private house, of course, a mansion on the height here, a garden on a gallery. I have it now, in her name. There was no challenge, there is none. Fickle as she always has been, my own behaviour is close enough to make a match with hers.

They asked what they should call me, in this hiatus between the nameless Pure that she was and the dragon that she means to be. It was her own blistering bitterness that said, "Find out what name the last tourist had, that used this decant. That'll do."

They did that, and so she is called Carnelia, and so am I.

They barely know that, down on the Row. She doesn't want to go out, to show them what she is. No more do I; there never has been any streak of cruelty in me, though I was always ruthless when I needed to be. When my art demanded it. I remember that.

I barely need the drugs now, to play at being her. This has gone far beyond play, or artifice. I have her, sunk deep into me—or else I'm sunk so far in her, I can barely find myself. That last fling, there was so much of her in my mind, I think she got into my datastream, and the two of us are inextricable now.

Is that a metaphor? I'm uncertain. It's all data. I had muddled myself and her so thoroughly in my consciousness, why wouldn't that affect what went out through the 'chute, what came back?

Art is all metaphor, describing one thing in terms of another, of what it is not. My life has been my art, given to it; my art has been my life, exploiting what I did, what I felt, what I learned.

Art is . . .

Art is . . .

I can no longer remember what art is. I can quote myself, but never understand me.

Someone else's vengeance has its cost; this is what I've paid, in more than money. There is so much of Carnelia in here, I have lost some part of myself. She drowns me, unless she drowns me out; she is very loud in my head. Imperative.

This is what else I've paid, in part, in money: the Splice has her new clinic, halfway up the wall's climb from the Row, just where she wanted it. Neither high side nor Underside, she can service both now, though not me. She has all the resources she could want, for whatever fantastic aberration she or her clients can conceive; she can work pro bono, experiment as she pleases. She's secure.

What she doesn't have, she's lost the record of her unwitting, unwilling benefactress, the datastream that Tethys stole. I arranged everything about the clinic's move, ordered it on the kind of whim so often shown by Promethea and her earlier incarnations. Somehow, in the process, the crucial data-chip went missing.

The Splice most likely thinks I took it, but she can't say anything, of course, she cannot ask. For all she knows, Carnelia already is that poor trapped soul recovered, set free. She has no reason to imagine that I'd still be here, muddied, trapped myself. And she does know that I recently took an hour of both 'chutes' time, though she doesn't know why. Her best guess must be that I used it to send myself home and set free the woman I'd displaced—some degree poorer, evidently, but very far from destitute.

It might have been the smarter thing to do, but it wasn't possible any more. If I've lost my art, I've gained—oh, some part of another's mind, that unreachable quest that the art had only ever been a metaphor fumbling towards, that other people fumble for in love or children or more exotic ways to share.

Instead, I thought I had dealt justly with Rotten Row, insofar as it had looked to me for justice.

Her entourage had kept her assassin penned, ready for her sentence. This was Rotten Row; she could do as she pleased with the birdman.

This was Rotten Row; I could do as I pleased, with anyone. I sent my entourage away for the day and hired some curious tourists to assist me, their last day in the habitat. A closed wagon took some of us to the Upchute; another fetched some of us back from the Downchute. They're both misnamed, of course: you can send a datastream either way, from both.

When my hangers-on returned, they found I had a houseguest, a young man in a fresh decant, as Pure as can be measured. He does not speak, and has trouble with clothes; spends most of his days crouched silent, naked in a corner of his room. I have servants hired specially to care for him, for as long as he needs them, as long as it takes.

Also, they found that my justice on the birdman is—to keep him just exactly as he is, some seeming pet in my seeming cruelty. Crippled and caged, the creature flaps scarred and flightless wings in my long garden, and screams in a voice so broken it's hardly any disturbance at all.

Sometimes I go just to sit, to look. No more than that; I do not speak. I have nothing to say to that soul, if indeed there's any soul still in there. My silence is an echo of that screaming, an utter lack of words to express my fury, my betrayal, my abandonment. This is my own revenge, which carries its own cost; something in me still dislikes being someone who would do this thing. But there's too much of her now, and she's done the like too often; I feel her flinch inside me, unless it's I who flinch from the desperate soul behind the birdman's eyes.

Well, that soul shall stay there. I spend more time with my unhappy houseguest, trying to coax him back into a semblance of humanity. One little touch at a time.

Mel I have not heard from, nor do I ask. I sent her the promised share of money, and more for Tethys, and for Dolph. She will likely be plotting her next decant with the Splice, now that she can afford her own adventures. I feel . . . nothing. This body may be meant for tourists, it may be primed for sex, but pheromones depend on contact and I keep far away, up here on the high side. I remember, but I do not understand my own previous passion.

Every revenge, my own or other people's, has its costs. I think I have paid mine.

Let that, let this be an end to it.

Terminus.